Alfred Hitchcock's
Solve-Them-Yourself Mysteries

ALFRED HITCHCOCK'S

Solve-Them-Yourself

MYSTERIES

Illustrated by Fred Banbery

Random House · New York

Grateful acknowledgment is made to the editorial assistance of Robert Arthur.

Library of Congress catalog card number: 63-7818

Contents

Introduction   *vii*

1. The Mystery of the Five Sinister Thefts   3

2. The Mystery of the Seven Wrong Clocks   41

3. The Mystery of the Three Blind Mice   73

4. The Mystery of the Man Who Evaporated 129

5. The Mystery of the Four Quarters   171

Introduction

Good evening, and welcome to Alfred Hitchcock's Bureau of Investigation. We are now offering a special feature to the public—a book full of new, exciting stories of suspense and mystery on the self-service, solve-it-yourself plan for those who like to test their detective ability against some good, meaty clues.

On the other hand, for those of you who like to race after the evildoer with a "tallyho!" and a "there he goes!" we will handle all arrangements. You can enjoy the excitement of the chase and leave the clues to us. We will gather them up after you and arrange them all neatly in place.

If this were a preview of my next motion picture, I would now give you some tantalizing glimpses of the attractions to come. You would see a three-hundred-pound millionaire who lives in an imported castle and collects enemies for a hobby. You would meet a talking skeleton, three witches on broomsticks, and a clock that tells yesterday's time instead of today's. You would encounter a kidnapped—or should I say snake-napped?—snake, a stolen midget cane, and a pair of giant shoes that may or may not have walked off by themselves.

Nor would this exhaust the list of jolly entertainments and delicious delights I would let you glimpse. There would be a man who evaporates from a locked room, a house where all the furniture is built half-size, and seven clocks that tell outrageously wrong times with, if you will allow me to say so, straight faces.

Throughout the stories you will see that I have occasionally commented on the clues you may, or may not, have caught. I'm afraid I just can't resist saying something whenever I get the chance. You have undoubtedly noticed me popping up in my television programs to make a few appropriate remarks every time they let me. It seems to be a habit I simply cannot break.

One last word. Some of my fans have experimented with reading these stories aloud, having gathered the whole family around to take turns with the reading. Whoever spots a clue shouts "Clue!" and wins a point. Then the group discusses whether or not it is a clue and, if so, what it means.

This is a wonderful form of togetherness if you care to try it. But one thing I do beg of you. Adhere to the stern code of the mystery reader. Don't reveal the answers to anyone when you have read the stories. Make your friends learn the solutions the hard way. See that they read the stories too!   —*Alfred Hitchcock*

The Mystery of the Five Sinister Thefts

ALFRED HITCHCOCK SPEAKING: *I trust that you like circuses. When I was a boy—yes, though you may find it difficult to believe, I was once a boy—every right-thinking lad aspired either to join a circus, or to become a detective like Sherlock Holmes. I couldn't make up my mind which I wanted most, with the result—well, you know how I wound up. No need to go into that. But now you may do both— join a circus and play detective—without ever leaving the comfort of your own easy chair. Just keep your eyes and ears alert for clues as we join Jerry Mason in ——*

The Mystery of the Five Sinister Thefts

JERRY HADN'T WALKED fifty feet up the rutted dirt road that led from the highway toward the tents and trailers of Clanton's Circus before he realized that something was wrong.

He was approaching the circus from the back, not from the main entrance, and everything looked exactly as it had an hour earlier when he left to take the bus to town to mail his Uncle Frank's registered letter.

Just the same, something was wrong.

Tall and thin, with blond hair that wouldn't stay combed, Jerry Mason liked to puzzle out anything that bothered him. Now he stopped and studied the little circus carefully.

Farthest from him was the lollipop-striped main tent where the big show was given every afternoon and evening. From the top of the main tent flew a banner that lazily opened to say CLANTON'S CIRCUS. Jerry never saw it without a thrill of pride. This was the first summer his parents had let him travel with the circus. It was also the first summer his Uncle Frank had actually owned it. For years Frank Mason had been Mr. Claypoole Clanton's gaffer, or general manager. But the past winter Mr. Clanton had retired, and Jerry's uncle had used his savings to buy the circus.

There was a lot of hard work connected with a circus, work that the customers never knew about. As a sort of general helper, Jerry was expected to lend a hand anywhere he was needed. This included assisting his uncle with the bookkeeping. As a special favor he was allowed to appear in the group clown acts. It was unusual for a "first of May"—a newcomer or greenhorn—to be allowed to be a Joey, or clown, but Jerry was tolerated by the older Joeys because he was helpful, likable, and didn't get in the way.

Now, even after one summer, he felt like a born circus man. His biggest ambition was to have the others in the circus treat him like one, instead of with the aloofness most of them gave to every first of May.

Jerry studied the circus carefully. Near the main tent, the big top, was the blue-and-white sideshow tent, and across from it the red animal tent. Then came the cook tent and the tent where the roustabouts slept. Then came the trailers and trucks which carried all of the people who, together, made up the little world of Clanton's Circus. It was only a one-ring circus, but as far as Jerry was concerned it was the best *little* circus in the United States.

Altogether there were thirty-seven more or less battered

trailers parked in a ragged double row between him and the big top. Jerry had counted them the first day he joined the circus. Where space permitted they were parked in a circle, but here, where the circus lot outside Green City narrowed at the rear, they were parked alongside the access road. All of the acts had their own trailers. So did the sideshow people. He and Uncle Frank shared a big trailer that also served as an office for the circus.

Jerry started walking again slowly, still puzzled. He couldn't see a thing unusual anywhere. And yet that strange feeling of something very wrong kept bothering him.

Suddenly he knew what it was—everything was much too quiet.

By this time on a bright August morning, the circus lot should be humming with sound. He ought to be hearing the thud-thud of the hammer gang driving tent stakes in more deeply, the throaty cough of one of the lions, the trumpeting of an elephant, the hum of conversations, and a dozen other distinctive sounds that mark a circus lot gradually getting ready for the big afternoon matinée.

Instead, there was comparative silence. Oh, there were sounds, of course, but not nearly enough.

And the near silence had an ominous quality about it. Of tension. Even of fear.

As Jerry reached the nearest parked trailer, he became aware that a number of the occupants were standing outside their trailers. All of them were looking in the same direction—toward the big top, or toward his uncle's trailer, which was parked near it.

Mr. Knott was standing in the grass beside his trailer, looking intent. Mr. Knott was a contortionist, who billed himself as *Mr. Knott, the Human Knot.* He happened to be standing on his hands, with his legs swung up behind him so that his feet dropped down over his shoulders and alongside his chin. He had been in show business for thirty years and had to practice a great deal to keep his muscles limber.

"Mr. Knott," Jerry said anxiously, "what's happened? Is anything wrong?"

Mr. Knott just shook his head briefly to show he didn't know. Then slowly he unwound himself to stand on his feet again.

Jerry began to hurry. Across the street was the trailer belonging to Cowboy Anderson, the lariat expert. A tall, lanky man, Cowboy was throwing a loop at a pole quite a distance away. To Jerry's amazement, he missed and pulled in his rope without even seeming to notice. His gaze also was fixed on the office trailer. Jerry had heard that the lariat expert had a sick wife in the hospital to whom he sent all of his pay.

Beyond Cowboy Anderson was the trailer belonging to Imo and Jimo, the silent, unsmiling pair of Japanese jugglers who stood now with Indian clubs in their hands, forgetting to practice, as they, too, looked up the road.

Opposite them were Achmed and Abdullah, the Acrobatic Arabs. Abdullah stood with feet apart and braced. On his head he balanced a six-foot aluminum pole with rubber cups at each end. On top of the four-inch-thick pole was Achmed, balanced upside-down on his head. As Jerry came opposite them, Achmed lost his balance and fell. He turned over in mid-air and landed on his feet. The pole fell with a dull thud almost on Abdullah's toes, a bit of clumsiness which ordinarily would have sent the swarthy little man into a fury of strange, hissing language that might actually be Arabic. But he didn't even seem to notice. He quickly grabbed the pole and, holding it tightly in one hand, looked up the road, like the others.

Outside the next trailer, an unusually large one, stood Biggo, the sideshow giant, and Major Mite, the midget. Biggo was eight feet one inch tall and wore size twenty-two shoes. He had a long face with an expression that always seemed to be asking a question.

Beside him Major Mite looked like a child. The major stood thirty-eight inches tall and weighed forty-one pounds. Rings glittering with diamonds sparkled on both his small, pudgy hands, and he always dressed like a tiny fashion model. Circus gossip said he was heavily in debt for his clothes and jewelry. Nevertheless, after he had worn a suit for a couple of months, he threw it away.

Major Mite never appeared without his cane, a short, polished stick with a crook handle which he used to get attention by tugging with it at someone's arm.

Now Major Mite impatiently tugged at Biggo's elbow.

"Biggo, you useless hulk," he said in a high, shrill voice, "lift me up. I can't see anything down here!"

"Nothing to see," Biggo grumbled, but he cupped his hands. Major Mite stepped in them, Biggo lifted him up, and Major Mite stepped onto his broad shoulders. There he stood as if on an observation tower, balancing himself by grasping Biggo's coarse black hair.

"What's happened?" Jerry called out. "Has there been an accident?"

Biggo shook his head, which almost made Major Mite lose his balance.

"Hold still, you human ox!" he shrieked. "You want to kill me?" The two were always quarreling; yet they traveled together and neither of them was happy if the other one was very far away.

"It's Jerry," the giant said.

"I can see it's Jerry. I've got eyes, haven't I?" Major

Mite snapped.

He looked down at Jerry. It gave him a great deal of satisfaction to be able to look down at normal people from Biggo's shoulders. As he said, it was very monotonous to spend your life looking up at everyone else.

"We heard someone screaming," he told Jerry, "but when we came out they'd stopped."

"I bet something else has been stolen," Biggo rumbled. "If it has I'm getting out of here. I'm quitting, you hear?"

"Oh, no, you're not," Major Mite told him. "Not until I get my cane back. My best cane, my lucky cane, the one I broke into show biz with. And you want your shoes back, don't you? Your best pair of handmade shoes?"

"I'm quitting," Biggo said doggedly. "Never mind about the cane or the shoes."

Jerry was already hurrying on. It would be bad news for his uncle if Biggo and Major Mite left the circus. They were very popular attractions.

He was just about to break into a run when someone called, "Jerry!" He stopped abruptly and turned to see an ancient little woman with a wrinkled face and twinkling eyes standing almost hidden by a trailer. It was Fortunata, the fortuneteller, wearing bright gypsy clothes. On her arm perched a trained mynah bird, which cocked its head to look at Jerry.

"Trouble!" the mynah bird, whose name was Mr. Dark, croaked. "I see trouble."

"Hush-a yourself," Fortunata scolded. "You're just a bird. But maybe," she said to Jerry, "we do have-a more trouble. Something's wrong for Madame Winifred."

"The snake charmer?" Jerry asked. "Is she sick?"

"Trouble!" croaked Mr. Dark again.

"No woman who yell-a so loud can be sick," Fortunata said, her smile vanishing. "She upset. Very upset. She's-a in

your uncle's trailer now. I think-a something more been stolen."

"Golly, I hope not!" Jerry exclaimed. "I better see if I can help Uncle Frank."

He started on the run for his Uncle Frank's trailer, passing the Six Flying Ferdinands, the circus' famous aerial act, and Sabre, the silent, gloomy sword swallower. All of them were uneasily looking toward the now silent trailer. Jerry reached it and burst in, breathing hard.

His Uncle Frank was sitting behind his desk, his weather-reddened features looking grim. Opposite him sat Madame Winifred, the plump snake charmer, who was called the Queen of the Serpents. Although in the gaudy banners that advertised her Madame Winifred was shown literally encircled by snakes, she was really a very nice person who liked to knit sweaters for her friends. The only thing unusual about her now was the snake coiled around her left arm like a huge bracelet, its head close to her cheek.

"Jerry!" she cried, turning toward him. "Have you seen her? Tell me that you know where my darling Belle is!"

"Belle?" Jerry blinked, trying to remember someone named Belle.

"My snake, Belle!" Madame Winifred choked. "My beautiful Belle, with her lovely white skin and black markings, my oldest friend, my dearest companion, taken from me. Stolen!" She liked to talk about her snakes as if they were people.

"Stolen!" Jerry gulped and sat down. Another strange theft! "Are you sure?"

"That's just what I was asking," Uncle Frank said gruffly. He leaned forward. "Winifred, you know how snakes can slip away through even a small hole. Maybe Belle——"

"No! It's impossible!" Madame Winifred wailed. "There's

only one window and it has heavy mesh over it. Somebody cut the mesh and stole Belle. Go look for yourself."

Frank Mason stood up. So did Jerry.

"I guess we'd better," Jerry's uncle said. "Winifred, you sit here and compose yourself. We'll find Belle if it's humanly possible."

They left her sitting there and ducked behind the trailer, ignoring the stares focused on them.

"Jerry, this is a bad business," his uncle said seriously as they moved toward the olive-green trailer that said MADAME WINIFRED on the side. "I wonder if a maniac is loose in this circus? Five nights ago somebody stole Biggo's best pair of shoes. Then the next night they stole Major Mite's lucky cane. The following night, Cowboy Anderson's prize roping lariat disappeared, and the next night they took one of Sabre's swords. And now a snake! It just doesn't make sense."

Jerry was silent. He was trying, without success, to imagine why anyone would steal such an odd assortment of things of no real value. Also, he was remembering what Uncle Frank hadn't mentioned—the theft of the diamond called The Green Flame. Worth almost $100,000, it had been stolen from the Museum of Fine Arts when the circus played Millerton five days earlier. But he didn't have time to ponder the past thefts any more at the moment, for they had reached Madame Winifred's trailer.

His Uncle Frank led the way up the little stairs and inside, ducking his head. They ignored the front half of the trailer, which had been turned into cozy living quarters, and turned to the rear. A metal door blocked it off. Behind this was another door of heavy wire mesh, and beyond the wire mesh were seven or eight glass tanks in which various richly colored snakes lay coiled.

One was a good-sized rock python, which lifted its head.

Jerry at first had been uneasy in the presence of the snakes, but he had quickly learned that they were all of harmless varieties, and all were extremely tame.

Frank Mason cast a quick look around.

"She's right," he said to Jerry. "Belle couldn't have slipped out. Winifred keeps these pets locked up tight because so many people worry about snakes. But look back there—the mesh over the ventilation window has been cut."

The only window was a small one, less than eighteen inches square, at the rear of the trailer, near the top. The wire mesh over it had been cut around the edges.

"We'll have a look from the outside," Jerry's uncle said.

Outside they found that the high window of the trailer was higher even than Frank Mason's head.

"Stand on my shoulders and look in," he told Jerry. But as he cupped his hands for Jerry, the boy gave an exclamation.

"Look!" he said.

There, directly below the window, in a sandy spot, was the outline of a footprint. It was a giant footprint, nearly twice the size of any normal human's.

"Biggo's footprint!" his uncle said. "That giant was here last night."

"Or else——" Jerry began and stopped. He wasn't quite sure what to think, at this point. "Let's see if I can find any more clues around the window."

The man hoisted him up and Jerry steadied himself and looked through the trailer window. The wire screen had been cut on two sides and at the bottom so the mesh could be pushed inward. Jerry got his head and shoulders through. Below him, out of reach, were the snakes—with one empty glass tank where, undoubtedly, Belle had been resting when she had been kidnapped—or rather, "snakenapped." There was no sign of any disturbance, and no other clues he could see.

He pulled back and dropped to the ground.

"Well?" Uncle Frank asked.

"Biggo couldn't have done it," Jerry said. "He couldn't get his shoulders through the window. Besides, he hates snakes. He says they give him the creeps."

"Biggo couldn't get through the window," Uncle Frank snapped, "but Major Mite could. You've seen how he rides around on Biggo's shoulder. He could lean through that window easily."

"But his arms are way too short," Jerry objected. "He couldn't reach down to pick up Belle."

His uncle chewed his lip.

"His cane!" he said. "He always tugs at people with it. He could easily have used the crook to catch Belle around the middle and lift her up. That's how it must have been done. Biggo and the midget working together!"

"But Uncle Frank," Jerry protested, "a pair of Biggo's shoes were stolen. So was the Major's lucky cane. They were both very upset. Someone else could have put on the giant shoes and used the cane to steal Belle, to make us suspect the wrong people."

His uncle chewed his lip again; his face looked troubled. The theft of some giant shoes and a cane and a lariat and an old sword, and now a snake, might not seem serious, but it was. It was serious because the seemingly senseless thefts had created an air of suspicion and anxiety which had enveloped the whole of the tight little world that was Clanton's Circus.

"Maybe you're right," he finally agreed. "And maybe Biggo and the Major just said the shoes and the cane were stolen."

"But what about Cowboy Anderson's lariat? And Sabre's sword?" Jerry asked.

"The midget could have slipped into their trailers and stolen them," his uncle suggested. "I bet the sword was used to cut that screen. And maybe the lariat was used to tie up the box or trunk or whatever it is they've used to hide Belle."

"But why?" Jerry asked, unwilling to think that Biggo and Major Mite could be guilty.

"I don't know. Maybe they're trying to confuse that insurance detective. Or make us forget about the diamond somebody stole back in Millerton. We'll learn the motive when we find the snake. I'm going to have the whole circus searched, from cook tent to the big top, inch by inch. And I'm going to give special attention to the trailer that belongs to Biggo and the major!"

"Please don't let them know you suspect them," Jerry said. "Biggo is threatening to leave the show as it is. He's very upset."

"Everybody's upset," his uncle said, taking long strides back toward the office trailer. "And if we don't find Belle, a lot of people will leave us. Maybe enough to ruin the show. This thing has got to be solved or we might get a reputation for being jinxed. Then I might as well say good-by to the money I invested in this circus!"

They got back to the trailer to find Madame Winifred cooing to the snake on her left arm. She looked up hopefully.

"Did you find Belle?" she asked.

"No, but we will," Frank Mason promised. "How big was she?"

"Seventy-one inches from nose to toes, if she had any toes," Winifred said. "Three and a half inches through the middle. And the nicest disposition of any snake I ever had. Of course, she's getting old now, and I don't use her in the act, but I still love her."

"We're going to hunt for her," the circus owner promised. "You go back to your trailer and get ready for the afternoon show."

"I'll give Hercules, the big python, a bath," Winifred decided, starting out. "And I'll boil up some eggs for my darlings. They aren't due to be fed until Sunday, but it'll help us all forget about poor Belle if I feed them today."

She went out. Jerry's uncle heaved a sigh.

"The way she feels about that snake would be funny if it wasn't so serious to her," he said. "Jerry, can you find that detective, Parker, and send him to me? I'm going to get Jake Farrell and a couple of others I can trust and organize searching parties. We'll look into every trunk, every suitcase, every box or barrel or sack or any place else where a snake as big as Belle could be hidden. And if we don't find her . . . Well, we've just got to find her."

"I'll get Parker," Jerry said. "May I help hunt, Uncle Frank?"

"Sorry, Jerry. We'll be searching right up to show time. I'll need you to keep an eye on the office. Grab a bite at the cook tent before you come back."

As Jerry went out into the bright sunshine, he was aware that something intangible in the atmosphere of Clanton's Circus had changed again. It was noisy once more—but there seemed to be a nervousness under the noise. Undoubtedly, by now everyone on the lot knew that one of Winifred's snakes had been stolen, and everyone was discussing the theft and trying to decide what it meant. Many of them, like Biggo, were probably very upset, because circus people, Jerry had observed, had a tendency to be temperamental and to believe in jinxes and hoodoos. As his uncle had said, if the circus got a reputation for being jinxed, he might as well write the circus off as a bad investment.

In that moment Jerry resolved he was going to solve the

strange mystery. He didn't know how, but he was going to do it.

Ahem. Pardon me for peeking over your shoulder, but I see Jerry has resolved to solve the mystery of the sinister thefts and I wondered if you felt you could solve it before he did. Of course, if you've already solved it, I'm going to feel rather dashed. But so many of you insist on guessing the ending of some of my best television shows that I've learned to beware of active young imaginations. Assuming, though, that you are not quite ready to handcuff the proper suspects, let me urge you to pay full attention to all that follows. Oh, and it wouldn't do any harm to go back over the events up to this moment. There have been at least two intriguing clues so far.

Jerry finally found Mr. Parker in the cook tent. The insurance detective had joined the show after the disappearance in Millerton the week before of the big diamond, The Green Flame. Parker, who was a baldish, thin little man with big ears, was posing as a newspaper reporter collecting material for some articles on circus life. He liked to sit in the cook tent and listen to the yarns of Paddy O'Reilly. Paddy had once done a strong man act, but he liked to eat so well that he got enormously fat. He gave up being a strong man and became a cook, which enabled him to eat all the scoffins he wanted.

Parker was sitting at a counter drinking coffee while Paddy told him stories of the old days when circuses traveled all over America.

"'Tis a sad thing to see the circus disappear, little by little, from this fine land," Paddy was saying sorrowfully. "When I was a lad just starting to kick sawdust—that means to follow the circus," he added, as Parker took furious notes, "'tis true there were plenty of grifters with every circus. We even used to have Monday men with the shows. Monday men were thieves, I won't mince words, permitted to steal only from clotheslines in the towns where the show played. But Clanton's Circus ain't like that. We went Sunday school long ago—abolished all the grift. That's why you won't find the fella who stole that diamond in Clanton's Circus now."

"How did you know I was looking for the diamond?" Parker demanded, upset because he thought his disguise was perfect, although everyone in the show had long since guessed what he was. Paddy looked abashed, but he was saved from having to answer when Parker saw Jerry and jumped up.

"Hey, kid," he said, "I want to talk to you."

That suited Jerry fine. He got a plate of stew and he and the detective moved to the end of the counter, where they wouldn't be overheard.

"Look, kid," Parker said, "I got a proposition. You get all over the circus, you hear people talk. Maybe you have some idea now who stole The Green Flame from that museum in Millerton." He sighed. "I can't get people to talk. I guess they must have figured out I'm a detective. But if you can help me recover the diamond, I'll split the reward with you. Five thousand dollars—or aces, as you call them in circus lingo."

"I know," Jerry said, thinking furiously. If Parker were a better detective, he would have realized that Clanton's Circus, except for a few of the people, still considered Jerry just a first of May. He wouldn't win their confidence until he had been around long enough to be considered an old-timer, or had done something special to prove that he was "with it"—really one of them.

If someone in the circus had stolen the diamond, however, Jerry wanted the thief found to clear the circus' good name.

"Why're you so positive it was someone with Clanton's Circus who took The Green Flame?" he asked.

"Because it stands to reason," Parker said promptly. "Look, kid, the circus lot back in Millerton is less than a quarter of a mile from the Millerton Museum of Fine Arts. Last Saturday morning, while you fellows were setting up the tents, somebody climbed the ivy in the back of the museum, got in a second-story window, and broke open the glass case where The Green Flame was on exhibit with a lot of other examples of fine Oriental workmanship. The diamond was set in the center of a big gold breastplate from India, and that's the only thing the thief took. It was a professional job—an amateur would have stuffed a lot of other things in his pockets. But the diamond was the only valuable article a thief could hope to get rid of."

"Yes, and you and the police right away jumped to the conclusion someone in the circus was responsible," Jerry retorted. "Just as soon as it was discovered missing. And the police came out and searched the whole show—every tent, every truck, every trailer, and all the people, too. We had to cancel the matinée and Uncle Frank lost a lot of money. Everybody was pretty angry, too."

"Except somebody who was scared," Parker retorted. "Somebody pried the stone out of the gold setting and threw the setting in the bushes. The police found it right beyond the tents. Obviously the diamond was much easier to hide than the big gold breastplate. Well, that's why I'm here—because the police couldn't find it. I'm positive the thief is right here on this circus lot and has the diamond somewhere close by."

"I'm afraid you're right," Jerry said reluctantly. "I'll help if you'll——"

"That's great, kid," Parker said warmly. "Now I'll tell you what I——"

"Wait a minute, you didn't let me finish. I was going to say I'd help you if you'll help us find Belle."

"Belle? Belle who?"

"Belle's a snake. She belongs to Madame Winifred."

"A snake! Now wait a minute! I'm not fooling around with any snakes. If you people have a poisonous snake loose——"

"None of Madame Winifred's snakes are poisonous," Jerry told him. "Belle was stolen, just like the giant's shoes, the midget's cane, Cowboy's lariat and the sword swallower's sword."

"Some whack having fun," Parker said darkly. "Count me out. I'm a people detective, not a snake detective."

"Look, Mr. Parker," Jerry said, losing his patience, "my uncle is organizing a search of the circus for Belle. He wants you to help. It'll give you a chance to look around for the diamond some more. Since you're a detective, you may think of some possible hiding places Uncle Frank's men would miss."

"Well, that's different," Parker agreed. He rubbed his chin. "Describe the missing person—I mean the missing snake."

"Seventy-one inches long, three and a half inches thick in the middle, with white skin and black markings, very gentle disposition," Jerry said. "In fact, she's a very old snake and rather feeble."

"Hmmm." Parker's gaze darted around the tent. "This is a new one. A snakenapping. Now where would you hide a snake? You know what? She'd just fit inside a spare tire, all coiled up. Or maybe inside a coil of fire hose."

"She's more likely to be in a box or trunk or basket,"

Jerry retorted. "Anyway, Uncle Frank wants everything searched. You better go report to him."

The detective hurried off, and Jerry finished his lunch, feeling very gloomy. Some of the circus people had begun to file in for an early lunch, and word of Belle's theft, and the impending search, was obviously on everybody's tongue. Paddy came over as he was finishing.

"So now it's a snake stolen," Paddy said grimly. "Jerry, I don't like it, I don't like it at all. What's this I hear we're all to be tumbled about in another search?"

Jerry nodded. "Belle has to be found."

"Well, at least they won't look for the lassie frozen into an ice cube in one of my refrigerators," Paddy grumbled. "That chief of police—he dumped all my ice out back in Millerton. And someone snitched a basket of boiled eggs from me. Now this. Jerry, I've seen good shows bust up over less than this."

Jerry nodded glumly and started back to the office trailer. He was so absorbed in his thoughts he scarcely heard or saw any of the bustling activity now going on around him until a hand touched his elbow.

"Jerry."

"Oh, Fortunata." It was the gypsy fortuneteller who had stopped him. On Fortunata's arm beady-eyed Mr. Dark stared at Jerry.

"Trouble!" he croaked. "Double, double, toil and trouble."

"We don't need-a you to tell us," Fortunata scolded him. "Jerry, you look worried."

"I am worried." Jerry told her what Paddy had said.

"Don't give up hope," Fortunata said. She took Jerry's arm. "Come, Mr. Dark tell-a your fortune."

She led the way to the small fortunetelling tent. Inside was a wooden table with six cages on it, and in each cage was a box full of folded slips of paper neatly stacked sidewise. The gypsy put Mr. Dark on the table and the bird waited expectantly.

"Mr. Dark, he wants a quarter," Fortunata chuckled. "A free fortune is-a no good. Must be paid for."

Jerry fished in his pocket and found a quarter. The mynah bird took it in its beak, walked over and dropped it into a green bowl. Then he started up a ramp to the cages. He was about to go in the middle cage when Fortunata whistled. Mr. Dark scurried on to the end cage, went in, picked out a piece of folded paper, and brought it to Jerry in his beak. Jerry took it, feeling puzzled, and read what was written on it. The message said:

To achieve your goal, you must think straight.

"Is-a good fortune?" Fortunata asked, black eyes twinkling.

Jerry nodded doubtfully.

"It's good advice, I guess," he said. "Though I don't see how it's any special help in this mess we're in."

"Mr. Dark give-a good advice, always. You think about it, Jerry."

If you'll excuse the intrusion, may I hopefully suggest we all take sixty seconds, not to listen to a commercial, but to think about Jerry's message? I have a feeling Fortunata and Mr. Dark are trying to tell Jerry something. Ah, but what? . . . Now back to our story.

Jerry found the office trailer empty. His uncle was out, busy on the search for Belle. Jerry dropped into the chair behind the desk, his head spinning with thoughts. Presently he reached for a piece of paper and a pencil and started writing. He liked to get his thoughts in order and writing them down was helpful. Maybe this was what Mr. Dark's message, *Think Straight,* had meant.

After a few minutes, he stopped to read what he had written, which was:

OBJECTS STOLEN

1. A valuable diamond.

2. A pair of giant shoes.

3. A midget cane.

4. A lariat.

5. A sword.

6. A snake.

QUESTION

Did the same person steal all of the above objects? If he did, why? What is the connection between a diamond, a pair of giant shoes, and the other objects? Or is there a connection between some of them and not between others?

Jerry stared at the paper. He could understand the theft of the diamond. But the other five thefts were so meaningless they seemed somehow sinister. Five sinister thefts! Then he remembered his conversation with Paddy. He scrawled another line:

Also reported stolen, a basket of boiled eggs.

This only made him feel more confused, though the eggs had probably just been stolen by somebody who was hungry. He was beginning to despair of ever making sense of the riddle when his uncle came in, looking dejected.

"Well, we didn't find the snake," he said grimly. "We turned this circus upside down, too. Looked in every trunk, bag, or anywhere else a snake could be hidden. That detective, Parker! The man's an idiot! He wanted to look in all the spare tires, the band's bass drum, and inside the tubs the elephants stand on in their balancing act. And Paddy almost took a cleaver to him when he started digging into Paddy's barrels of flour and sugar."

He managed a chuckle at the recollection. Then he shook his head.

"I just don't know what to make of it, Jerry. All the years I've been with this circus, nothing so senseless ever happened. Everybody's on edge—nervy. The last time I recollect everyone feeling this way was in 'fifty, just before the hurricane. We had a blow-down then, and lost half our animals. Well . . . all we can do is go on with the show. Got to get ready for the matinée. We'll have to hurry, but——"

He turned in response to a knock on the door. Jake Farrell, his gaffer, a big red-headed man, came in. There was a strange look on Jake's normally good-natured face.

"Well, we found them," he said.

"You found Belle?" Jerry's uncle asked.

"Not Belle, no. But the other things. The shoes, the cane, that stuff."

"Where?"

"They were buried behind the cook tent. One of my men noticed evidence of digging and called me and—well, it's something you'd better see for yourself. Just as we found it."

Looking puzzled, Frank Mason followed him. Jerry tagged after them, anxious to know what could make someone like Jake Farrell seem so disturbed.

The circus lot was buzzing with activity now. The first townspeople were arriving and starting to buy balloons and spun-sugar candy and visit the animal tent and the side-shows. Inside the big top, last-minute preparations for the matinée were being made. Jake led Jerry and his uncle around behind the trailers, then behind the cook tent, where they saw several roustabouts staring down at a piece of canvas on the ground.

"Look, Mr. Mason," Jake said and lifted the canvas. Under it, in a hole in the soft earth, was a narrow black box that looked exactly like a miniature coffin. And driven through the lid, so that only the handle could be seen, was the sword swallower's missing sword.

"What the deuce!" his uncle exclaimed, but Jake was already picking the box up. He pulled the sword free and opened the lid. Jerry strained on his toes to peek in. And a queer thrill of horror ran down his spine.

Inside the miniature coffin were Biggo's missing shoes— slashed and cut by a sharp blade. Scattered over them were pieces of Major Mite's stolen cane. It had been broken into a dozen small pieces. Lying beside them was Cowboy's lariat. Someone had tied it in a hangman's knot, and inside the loop of the noose was a rag doll with a crude snake inked on its arm, obviously intended to portray Madame Winifred.

It looked as if someone, by burying these objects, was threatening the very lives of the owners.

"Get that out of sight!" Frank Mason said sharply, his face white. "Don't mention it to anyone."

Jake wrapped the piece of canvas around the black box. "Afraid it's too late." His tone was somber. "Several people saw us dig it up and the story's probably all over the lot by now."

"You men!" Frank Mason rapped out. "Back to your jobs. Jake, come with me—we have to have a conference. Jerry, better get ready for the matinée."

"Yes, Uncle Frank," Jerry said, his thoughts spinning wildly over the strangely upsetting contents of the buried box. He wished he could talk to his uncle for a moment.

No one had mentioned that, of all the objects stolen from the circus, only the snake Belle was still missing. Why should someone bury the other stolen objects in such a way they were bound to be found—but not the snake? Did the thief want the black box and its contents found? To Jerry it looked as if he did. But why? The net result would be to make everyone in the circus just that much more on edge and maybe ready to pull out and leave the show.

Was someone trying to ruin the circus? Was that the answer?

The question nagged at him all the way to clown alley— the clowns' make-up tent. Jacques, the head clown, a superb pantomimist who probably earned the biggest salary in the circus, was putting on his sad-tramp make-up and costume. He was aloof with Jerry, but not unfriendly, as befitted his position as a circus aristocrat.

"You're late, boy," he said.

"Yes, Mr. Jacques," Jerry answered, short of breath. He pulled on a red-and-white clown suit. Then he began to make up his face. He reddened his nose, put white circles around his eyes and gave himself huge red lips, outlined in white. It was a very simple make-up. It would be several years, if he stayed with the circus, before he could hope to work up an act and special make-up of his own.

"Next year, Mr. Jacques," he began, "can I be a Joey again? I know I'm awful young, but if you and the other Joeys don't mind my being around—well, I'd like to do it again."

"Mmmm." Jacques put on a wig out of which, later, firecrackers would shoot. "If there is a next year. For this show." He slid a live duck into his pocket, from which it would emerge unexpectedly later. "That business about the little coffin and the giant's shoes and the midget's cane and the other stuff is all over the place now. Everybody's jittery.

A lot of them think someone is putting a hoodoo on the show."

"Oh, no!" Jerry said in dismay.

"Several acts are ready to blow the stand, right now. Biggo and Major Mite for one. Madame Winifred for another, and Cowboy Anderson, too. Half the rest won't sign up for next year if they really get to believing there's a hoodoo on the show."

In silence Jerry finished his make-up. Somebody was certainly disrupting the whole circus, all right, with the curiously sinister thefts and the strangely upsetting method of burying the stolen objects, but he was convinced the culprit had a deeper motive than that. But what?

He had made no progress in figuring out any answers by the time he heard the band strike up its familiar music. He went racing after Jacques and the other Joeys into the big top.

For the next hour Jerry was too busy to do any thinking. During the clown parade he did cartwheels and backflips, at which he was very good. When the other Joeys did a special act, he stayed in the background.

As the other acts came on, he and the other clowns took up inconspicuous positions, ready to help if necessary. It was a tradition with Clanton's Circus that if some act had trouble, if there was an accident or something disrupted the performance, the clowns came to the rescue and distracted the audience's attention.

Today the show went badly, the worst Jerry had ever seen. With every minute that passed he felt all of the circus people getting more nervous. The feeling even communicated itself to the animals. Old Mom, the leader of the elephant herd, didn't want to do her dancing act, and when Old Mom wouldn't work, neither would any of the others. In the big cat act, the lions forgot their training and began to fight with one another until they were separated.

Imo and Jimo, the clever Japanese jugglers, started tossing lighted torches back and forth, a trick they could have done with their eyes blindfolded. But today they got rattled and Imo was badly burned by a torch that he misjudged.

Jerry covered for them by spinning cartwheels out into the ring until Achmed and Abdullah came running in for their precision tumbling and acrobatic act. Their acrobatics made the crowd gasp, but even they showed the effects of the general nervousness when they tried their big number, in which Achmed stood on his head at the end of the six-foot aluminum cylinder that Abdullah in turn balanced on his head. Even before he got himself into position, Achmed lost his balance and fell heavily. The aluminum cylinder thudded dully down on top of him.

Jerry gazed at them curiously, reminded of something, then joined the other clowns again in distracting the crowd. He heard the two Arabs hissing angry words to each other as they ran out, but now he was admiring the wizardry of Jacques, who completely in pantomine pretended to be two acrobats. He balanced an invisible companion on a long pole high above him so realistically that Jerry and the crowd could almost see him.

This helped to save the day while the riggers hastily erected the nets for the tremendous aerial act of the Flying Ferdinands. Watching them smoothly swing back and forth high in the air, Jerry began to hope things were getting back to normal. But just as he was beginning to relax a little, Signor Ferdinand, the head of the troupe, missed a catch of his wife doing a double back somersault. She fell into the net.

The entire crowd gave a horrified gasp of dismay as the net collapsed under her weight, due to faulty rigging. But she leaped up, showing that she was unhurt, and again the clowns were called upon to put on a show to cover the slip. The angry Ferdinands slid down and stalked out, not even taking their bows.

"They won't be back next year," Jacques said out of the side of his mouth, as Jerry pretended to slap his face, with the result that firecrackers exploded in his hair. "I'm sorry, kid, this show is finished. One of the candy butchers just told me that Cowboy Anderson has left, and Biggo and Major Mite tried to drive away and your uncle has gone down to nab them and hold them for arrest."

Mechanically, Jerry did a cartwheel. Biggo and Major Mite had nothing to do with all this. He was positive of it. Everything that had happened bore the mark of some very clever, malicious mind that worked with snakelike crookedness . . .

Snakelike crookedness! But snakes weren't always crooked!

And at that thought a lot of other thoughts that had been rattling around in Jerry's mind suddenly fell into place, like the last few pieces in a difficult jigsaw puzzle.

Suddenly he was sure he understood the meaning of—

A miniature coffin . . .

A stolen pair of shoes and cane . . .

A missing snake . . .

A nervous giant and dwarf who wanted to leave the circus immediately . . .

A vanished basket of hard-boiled eggs . . .

The fortune Mr. Dark had given him . . .

And a peculiar dull thud he had heard twice that day . . .

All these and other pieces of the puzzle now made sense to him. And Jerry knew he had to act before it was too late.

He backflipped to the center of the ring, where Jacques was pretending to be astounded by the fireworks in his fuzzy bright-red hair.

"I have to do something!" he whispered to the head clown. Without waiting for an answer, he cartwheeled toward the performers' entrance to the big top.

Once outside, he got to his feet and ran in the direction of the trailers.

The lot was almost deserted, with all the townspeople inside watching the show. But at the trailer shared by Biggo and Major Mite there was a commotion. Both the giant and the dwarf stood outside the trailer, shouting angrily to someone inside.

Jerry didn't stop.

On the other side of the road he saw the Flying Ferdinands grimly making preparations to blow the stand— leave the show. Cowboy Anderson's trailer was already gone.

But the shiny blue trailer Jerry was interested in was still there.

Two men, however, were in the car that pulled it, and the driver had just started the motor. Jerry ran around behind the trailer, out of their sight. The trailer had a rear door. He hoped it wasn't locked. He reached up, turned the handle, and the trailer door opened. Even as the trailer started to move he scrambled in and looked quickly over the apparatus which was stored in the rear section of the trailer. He saw what he wanted and grabbed it. The long object was heavy and hard to balance, but clasping it in both arms he jumped out and began to run back up the road with it. He hoped the men in the car wouldn't see him.

But they did.

The car stopped. The doors burst open and the two men shot out after him.

They yelled at him in angry voices, but he didn't pause. Lugging his clumsy burden, he ran as fast as he could.

Biggo and Major Mite were still outside their trailer, angrily shouting. He headed for them as the two pursuers gained on him.

"Biggo!" he yelled with the last of his breath. "Biggo! Help!"

Then, just before he reached the surprised giant, one of the running men tackled him. He went down, the object he was carrying went flying from his arms, his head hit something hard, and he blacked out.

Which seems like a good moment for me to pop up once more. I'll take the next sixty seconds while we wait for Jerry's head to clear to ask if you have solved the mystery of the sinister thefts yet? No—don't answer that. I'm afraid you will say yes, and I take a very dim view of young people who are smarter than I am. But for those of you who are still busy with their homework on this case, let me suggest that you ponder the following facts: there was only one reason for stealing Belle. There were two reasons for stealing the shoes, the cane, the lariat and the sword. A snake is not always crooked. And don't forget the dull thud . . . . A word to the wise is commonly supposed to be sufficient! Of course, if you just want the answer, full steam ahead, and I promise to make no more appearances until we sign off.

CONCLUSION

Jerry opened his eyes to find that his uncle was helping him sit up. Jake Farrell stood near by. Jerry blinked, and winced at the throbbing in his head. He could see Biggo firmly holding the two men who had chased him.

"Jerry, are you all right?" his uncle asked.

Jerry rubbed his head. "I guess so," he said. "It's just a bump."

"Then"—and his uncle's tone became grim as he helped Jerry to his feet—"I think you'd better start explaining, young man. These two claim you stole one of their props, and that you're the thief who stole Biggo's shoes, the Major's cane, and all the other things. Jerry, have you been playing boyish pranks, without stopping to think of the very serious consequences?"

"No, Uncle Frank!" Jerry said emphatically. "I did take that"—he pointed to the object that Jake Farrell was holding—"but I had to. I think I know what's been happening."

"Well, then I certainly hope you're going to tell the rest of us." His uncle's tone was a little softer.

"It'll be clearer if I go step by step," Jerry suggested. "From the beginning. It's really pretty simple——"

"Simple!" his uncle exclaimed.

"——once you understand how everything fits together."

"That's exactly what we want." His uncle looked around. Crowds of townspeople were streaming from the big top, where the show was over, and beginning to push past them.

"It'll be easier to talk in the trailer," Frank Mason said. "Let's go in. Biggo, bring those two."

The two men struggled, protesting, but Biggo's huge hands held them securely and marched them into the trailer. Soon they were all crowded in—Jerry and his uncle and Jake Farrell, Parker, the insurance detective, Biggo and Major Mite, looking puzzled, and the two men. It was a large trailer—it had to be to accommodate the huge bulk of the giant—so they all were able to find places. Biggo closed the door and sat against it. The two men subsided sullenly as Jerry began to speak.

"It all began five days ago in Millerton," he said, "when that diamond, The Green Flame, was stolen."

"I knew it. I always said so!" Parker exclaimed, and was silenced by a look from Frank Mason.

"The museum it was stolen from was close to the circus lot," Jerry continued. "Someone climbed up the ivy in back to the second floor windows. The robbery had all the marks of an experienced thief—or thieves."

"Just what I said!" Parker interjected.

"Well," Jerry went on, "the police of Millerton suspected Clanton's Circus right away, maybe just because we were strangers, and they immediately started a search of everybody, every tent and every trailer. I'm just telling what you all know," he added, "because that's how I kept the facts straight in my mind while I was trying to figure this whole thing out."

"Go on, boy," his uncle said quietly.

"Well," Jerry said, "the search threw the thief into a panic. He had to hide the diamond right away, and hide it somewhere no policeman on earth would ever think of looking. And he didn't dare hide it in his trailer because if it were found, it would be a dead giveaway that he was guilty. So he pried it out of the setting, threw away the setting, and hid the diamond."

"But where?" Jake Farrell asked, scowling.

"I'm going to come to that," Jerry promised. "But first, let me talk about the other thefts.

"The same night after the theft of The Green Flame, Biggo's shoes were stolen. That upset him very much."

"It sure did," the giant grumbled. "My best shoes. Cost me a hundred dollars to have them custom made!"

"The next night," Jerry continued, "Major Mite's cane was stolen."

"My lucky cane!" Major Mite shrilled excitedly. "The one I've had ever since I broke into show business. Money couldn't buy it. If I ever catch the scoundrel who broke it I'll wring his neck!"

And he clenched his tiny fists in a way that was almost comical. But no one smiled. Frank Mason merely nodded at Jerry to continue.

"Well, then came the theft of Sabre the sword swallower's sword and of Cowboy Anderson's best lariat," Jerry said. "It just didn't seem to make sense that anybody would steal such things."

"Sure it does," Parker said. "The thief used them to help him snakenap Belle."

"No." Jerry shook his head. "I mean, he used them, all right, but that was just an afterthought. He had two much better reasons for stealing such curious objects. The first reason was to get everybody in the circus upset and jittery. That's also the reason he buried the things in a miniature coffin. Just atmosphere. To make people think somebody was putting a hoodoo on the circus."

He looked at the frowning faces of the men around him. Even Major Mite's tiny face was wrinkled into a miniature mask of puzzlement.

"You see," Jerry continued, "all along the thief really

wanted to steal Madame Winifred's snake, Belle. Or I should say thieves, because it was plain it took two men to steal Belle, one lifting the other up. But after they got Belle, they wanted to leave the circus with her right away without arousing suspicion. By stealing the shoes and other things, they got people worked up to the point where several of the acts actually were going to leave the circus, and the thieves could go along without it seeming suspicious. Also, no one would guess that Belle really counted. Everybody figured the way the thieves wanted them to—that Belle was just part of the meaningless thievery. That was the second reason for the thefts."

"Wait a minute!" Frank Mason exclaimed. "You mean there's a connection between Belle and the stolen diamond?"

Jerry shook his head so hard the bump started hurting, and he winced.

"I'm sure of it," he said. "Especially since I learned from Paddy that the day the diamond was stolen a basket of hard-boiled eggs disappeared."

A curious expression came to Jake Farrell's face. "Wait a minute!" he said. "Let's see if I've figured what you're thinking." He looked around at the others. "Winifred feeds her snakes eggs," he said. "You've all seen her move the eggs around so they'll seem alive, then the snakes swallow them."

The others nodded, looking puzzled. Jake Farrell continued.

"Well, suppose someone who had just stolen a valuable diamond knew he was going to be searched in a minute, and had to hide the diamond where no one would dream of looking for it, but where he could get it back later. He saw Belle's trailer unattended. He thought of the snakes. He swiped some hard-boiled eggs from the cook tent in the confusion and——" He looked at Jerry. "You figured it out, Jerry. You finish it."

"What I think the thieves did," Jerry said, "was to dig a hole into a hard-boiled egg and push the diamond into the hole, after prying it loose from the setting. Then they fed the egg to Belle. They picked on Belle because she was just the right size to fit into the hiding place they had in mind for her later on."

"I'll be switched," Frank Mason said slowly. "Who ever heard of hiding a diamond in a snake? But it sounds logical."

"Of course," Jake Farrell told him. "Then later they had to steal the snake back without arousing suspicion. So they stole all the other things first to get us confused. But, Jerry, where is Belle hidden?"

Jerry picked up the aluminum rod that Achmed and Abdullah, the Acrobatic Arabs, used in their headstand balancing act.

"This is six feet long," he said, "and four inches in diameter. Belle is five feet eleven inches stretched out straight, and three and a half inches in diameter. For an aluminum pole, it's awful heavy and it doesn't seem to balance right. The dull thud when it fell, and Mr. Dark's fortune, made me think of it. And unless I'm wrong——"

With an effort he pulled off the big rubber cup at one end of the aluminum pole and lifted it up. As everyone watched, the missing Belle slid slowly out of the cylinder and fell limply on the floor.

Achmed and Abdullah made a scramble for the door, but Biggo was in front of it and they couldn't get past him. They were quickly silenced.

Frank Mason picked up the snake.

"Poor Belle," he said. "She's dead. Suffocated, I guess. But she was old and feeble, and we'll try to make up to

Madame Winifred for her. Anyway, it'll make it easier to test your guess, Jerry."

"And if you're right, boy," Parker, the detective, said importantly, "I'm going to cut you in on the reward money for the diamond—ten percent."

"You are, are you!" Jake Farrell roared. "It's Jerry who solved this thing. He gets any reward that's given!" And he turned to Jerry, holding out a hamlike paw.

"It'll help see you through college," he said. "Meanwhile, welcome to Clanton's Circus. You're no first of May, you're a real trouper, boy. You're with it!"

He engulfed Jerry's hand in his, and Jerry couldn't have asked for a better reward.

ALFRED HITCHCOCK SPEAKING: *I like to have the last word, so as we place The Mystery of the Five Sinister Thefts in the Closed file, let me say that poor Belle was, indeed, concealing the missing diamond. Snakes, it seems, have very lethargic digestive systems. Achmed and Abdullah later proved to be clever European jewel thieves who played circuses in summer to give themselves a respectable front, while during the winter they made off with all manner of baubles and sparklers. If you ask why they did not remove the diamond from Belle as soon as they had stolen her, the answer is evident. If Belle had been found with an incision through which the diamond had been removed, the whole plan might have been guessed. No, they had to take Belle and get away from the circus with her without their departure seeming suspicious.*

Oh, the dull thud which was mentioned? Well, Jerry saw Achmed and Abdullah fail twice in their special balancing act. He thought it was because of nervousness, but each time something about the mishap bothered him. Suddenly, after the second failure, he realized that when the pole fell it thudded dully, rather than giving off a metallic ring as it should have. This suggested that there was something in it, something soft which muffled the sound and also threw off the balance so that Achmed and Abdullah were unable to perform their act. The rest is, I trust, obvious. If you have any questions, however——

Oh, about Fortunata, Mr. Dark and the fortune? Jerry never could learn for sure whether the old gypsy knew more of the whole affair than she would admit. He suspected she knew what had really happened, but being a gypsy couldn't bring herself to inform on anyone. So she used a roundabout method to get Jerry's mind working along the right lines. After all, when you are looking for a missing snake coiled up in a trunk or a box or even a bass drum, you aren't apt to think of a snake stretched out straight and hidden in a hollow pole. Now, please, our space is up. The publisher simply insists we move on to the next case.

The Mystery of the Seven Wrong Clocks

ALFRED HITCHCOCK SPEAKING: *In the world of television, time comes in two standard sizes— the half hour and the hour. In everyday life, however, time is more flexible. It can crawl by like a snail going to the dentist. Or it can race past like an orbiting satellite. It can even turn backward—which is exactly what happens here. The clues are present. You are invited to turn detective and help solve——*

The Mystery of the Seven Wrong Clocks

THE HOWL THAT SOUNDED in his ear was so eerie and un-expected that Mr. Peter Perkins, puzzle and cryptogram editor of the *Sunday Morning Star,* stopped dead in his tracks. Gripping his gold-headed cane tightly, the dapper little man turned. In the dim shadows of the late October twilight, he was startled to see a bony white skeleton reaching for him, while a vampire bat soared at his face and a wolf crouched to leap.

Dear me, I'm afraid this situation seems a bit improbable, doesn't it? Confidentially, the above scene is known in television parlance as a "teaser." The meaning of the word, I trust, is self-evident. To make the whole thing clear, we will now take advantage of that flexibility of time which I just mentioned to turn the clock back a mere sixty seconds.

Peter Perkins, his velvet-lapelled topcoat tightly buttoned, a derby sitting with dignity atop his silvery locks, was strolling along the boardwalk at Atlantic Beach.

It was dusk, and the boardwalk was deserted except for him. The amusement park, which took up six blocks of the shoreline of the small city of Atlantic Beach, was silent and empty, filled only with the whispering ghosts of merry-makers long since gone. Actually, the whispering ghosts were only leaves, but the little puzzle editor had a lively imagination.

In summer, Atlantic Beach was a blaze of lights by sun-down. It roared with the laughter of surging crowds, the thunder of the roller coasters, the pop-pop-pop of shooting galleries. That was when Peter Perkins, who lived only a few blocks away, liked it best.

Tonight there was something curiously lonely about it. On Peter's left the Atlantic Ocean rolled up on the beach with a grumbling sound. Ahead of him the boardwalk vanished in the dusk like a wooden road to nowhere. To his right, the framework of the roller coaster rose against the sky like the bones of a vast dinosaur, and the Ferris wheel was a circular monster about to roll over and crush him.

In an effort to shake himself out of his strange mood, the puzzle editor stepped out more briskly. He intended to walk for twenty minutes, then go back to Atlantic Street, a block from the beach, and call on his old friend Fritz Sandoz, who had a watch and clock repair shop and was also a great puzzle enthusiast. They worked puzzles together one night a week.

Peter Perkins had taken only a dozen steps, however, when a long, mournful wail sounded in his ear.

He wheeled. And there in the twilight dimness he saw a skeleton reaching out for him, a vampire bat soaring at

him, and a wolf crouched to leap, licking its chops.

Of course, these fearsome creatures were only painted on the wooden front of the big building beside him, but that fact didn't cheer Peter Perkins up much. He was standing opposite the House of Terror, which advertised, *We are not responsible if your hair turns white.* The entire front of the building was covered with nerve-wracking paintings depicting some of the jolly entertainment to be found within. In the dim light, only half seen, they were much too real for comfort.

Then the mournful wail sounded again. It definitely seemed to come from within the House of Terror. Somehow a puppy had got into the building and was trapped.

Peter hesitated. The sensible thing to do was to call the police. But it was several blocks to the nearest telephone, and the police might be delayed. The pup howled again, sounding so lonely and frightened that Peter Perkins made up his mind. He would see if he could let the dog out himself. He was too fond of animals to make it stay in there all alone any longer than necessary.

The wooden door leading into the House of Terror was locked. But it was an old door and the wood had shrunk. He could see the metal tongue which held it shut, between the door and the jamb. Peter Perkins, who knew a great many odd things, knew how to deal with a lock like this. And under the circumstances he was sure no one would disapprove. He gave his penknife a sideways push with the point imbedded in the softer metal of the lock, and the brass tongue eased out of its socket. The door swung open. A draft of cold, damp air blew in Peter's face. But the little man was not timid. He strode inside, into inky darkness, closing the door behind him, and felt along the wall for a light switch.

"Here, boy," he called reassuringly. "Here, boy."

The dog howled again; he sounded farther away now. Then Peter found a switch. A light came on, for the owner kept the power on so he could inspect the premises during the winter and make sure none of the delicate electronic apparatus which was used in the House of Terror had suffered damage.

The light that came on was not, however, the bright overhead light Peter expected. Instead, it was a pale blue spotlight and it shone down on a niche in the wall, illuminating a skeleton that raised its bony finger and pointed at him.

"Welcome," the skeleton said in a ghostly voice. "If you insist on being foolish, follow the footprints. If your act has *grave* consequences, the management disclaims all responsibility."

Peter knew perfectly well that the skeleton was made of plastic, that the voice came from a magnetic tape, and that the lighting was controlled by an automatic switchboard. Nevertheless, all alone in the darkness, he felt he would like to hear the sound of a real human voice—even if only his own.

"Do you know Walter?" he asked the skeleton.

It was a joke he was publishing the following Sunday. The skeleton should have asked, "Walter who?"—whereupon Peter would have answered, "Walter-wall carpeting."

Instead the skeleton gave a weird laugh and vanished. A long line of footprints appeared on the floor, leading off into the darkness, each one a clearly outlined patch of light.

Peter Perkins was not sure he liked the idea of investigating the dark building, but the dog howled again, a long, pitiful, heart-rending wail that made up his mind for him.

"All right, boy," Peter called. "I'll come find you."

He strode forward, following the glowing footprints, for he

knew they would lead him on a safe path through the darkness. He went through a door and there was a wild shriek. Lightning flashed, thunder rumbled, and three witches on broomsticks sailed up past his nose.

He smiled, rather weakly, and went on. In the next room a flock of vampire bats circled his head. He resisted the impulse to duck, because he knew they were on wires. But when, in the next room, some ghostly figures stretched out white-shrouded arms for him, he had to stop to remind himself they were only cheesecloth on wires, painted with a special paint that became visible only under ultraviolet light. Even so his heart was beating faster than normal, and in order to steady his nerves, he asked the ghosts one of his favorite riddles.

"Why didn't Noah's family play cards on the ark?" he asked.

Instead of answering, the ghosts moaned dismally. So Peter gave them the answer.

"Because Noah was sitting on the deck," he said.

At that the ghosts gave a wild scream and shot upward, to disappear. Reflecting on the curious way paint and invisible light could affect one's nerves, Peter Perkins walked rapidly onward, calling out, "Here, boy! Here, boy!"

He passed through a room where dozens of wax figures of well-known murderers stood in frozen replica of their crimes, and then through another room where with a horrible shriek a figure with a rope around its neck fell through a trap door.

There were other rooms, equally ingenious, but by now Peter had his nerves under good control. He kept calling the dog but, to his puzzlement, the dog's howls never got any closer. At last he came to the exit, which he knew opened on an alley at the rear of the building, and very much baffled he let himself out.

For a moment he stood blinking in the darkness of the deserted alley. Opposite him were the backs of the shops and buildings that fronted on Atlantic Street, the main street of the town. And just a few feet away, tied up in someone's back yard, was a puppy. When it saw him, it howled again—a melancholy howl of vast loneliness.

"So you're the villain, eh, boy?" Peter Perkins murmured. When the puppy howled, the sound was caught by the intake of the ventilation system of the House of Terror. Given strange quivery additions by the big ventilating pipes, the howl had sounded all through the building and had emerged from the exhaust pipe at the boardwalk, where Peter had first heard it.

"You gave me quite a start," Peter said. "Sorry I can't turn you loose but you'd run away."

It had been an interesting adventure, and it had almost brought him to the place he had originally been headed for—Fritz Sandoz' Clock Hospital. Fritz, a little wizened gnome of a Swiss, was a wizard at repairing any kind of clock. He and Peter had been good friends for years. The back of the shop was just a few feet down the alley. Peter walked to it and opened the rear door.

He did not knock because Fritz was somewhat deaf; he was also totally dumb, due to an accident that had occurred when he was a young man in the Swiss Army. But the rear door had a special lock. If you turned the knob three times to the right, four times to the left and twice back to the right, it opened. Peter, who knew the combination, walked into a dark room and called out.

"Fritz? Fritz?"

A voice roared in his ear, "I've got you!" Huge hands grabbed him. Helpless as a baby, Peter Perkins was dragged into the back room of the Clock Hospital, where lights blazed brightly.

"I caught the killer," a deep voice said in his ear, "returning to the scene of the crime."

Peter Perkins blinked as his eyes adjusted.

In front of him he saw Detective Sergeant Magrue, of the local police force. Two other men were bending over something on the floor a few feet away, at the foot of a fine old grandfather's clock, one of the many clocks of all shapes and sizes which Fritz Sandoz collected.

And then, with a shock of horror, Peter Perkins saw what the men were bending over. It was his old friend, the wizened little clockmaker, Fritz. And he knew—there could be no doubt of it—that Fritz was dead.

His gaze came back to the bulldog features of Detective Magrue, whom he knew from the past. Magrue looked at him with glowering dislike.

"Let him go, Snider," he said. "That's Peter Perkins, the puzzle pest. He's a nuisance, but I don't guess he's a killer."

"But he came right in the back door," the policeman who had grabbed Peter protested. "And you said to keep an eye out for the criminal returning to the scene of the crime. . . ."

"Forget it," Detective Magrue said. "Go help the others. Perkins!" He fixed the little puzzle editor with a steely eye. "What are you doing here, sneaking in the back way?"

"I wasn't sneaking in," Peter Perkins told him. "I was coming to see Fritz. We were going to work puzzles together."

"Work puzzles together?" Magrue's heavy eyebrows drew together.

"Fritz was a very good puzzle solver," Peter said. "He and I both belong to the National Puzzle League. He was Cicero and I'm Plutarch!"

"Cicero!" Magrue said. "Plutarch! Perkins, you'll kill me

yet with all your nonsense."

"Those are club names," Peter told him with dignity.

"Well, this is no puzzle game," Magrue said. "This is murder. And I don't want any interference from you. Do I make myself clear?"

Magrue was referring to the fact that several times in the past Peter Perkins had given him suggestions on difficult cases. Some of the suggestions had been good ones, which had only made Magrue angrier.

"Who killed him?" Peter asked. "Who killed Fritz?" He tried to keep his voice steady but was not successful.

"That's what I'm here to find out," Magrue said. "It happened last night. He was in here, winding his clocks, as anybody can see, so that means it had to be midnight—he wound his clocks at midnight every night on the dot."

Peter nodded. That was true.

"Someone slipped in, using a duplicate key—anyway, the door wasn't forced. Because of his deafness, Fritz couldn't hear the intruder. He slipped up behind Fritz and—well, he hit him over the head. We know that much. It'll help some in running the fellow down."

"It had to be someone who knew him," Peter said. "And knew that he distrusted banks and kept all his money in a secret drawer of his desk. He didn't have any enemies so it had to be someone who did it for money."

"That much we figured," Magrue growled. "Seeing as how the drawers of his desk were jimmied open. Now we don't need any help from puzzle-nutty amateurs, so you can just beat it and . . . No." He changed his mind. "You go sit in his office, just in case I need to ask any questions. Sit there. And don't touch anything!"

Peter Perkins wanted to ask many questions. But he knew Magrue's temper. Silently he walked to the little office and workshop which opened off the big back room.

It was a small room cluttered with clocks, most of them taken apart, and with watches laid out on a bench for future work. There was a desk and, as Magrue had said, the drawers had been forced open by a thief looking for the savings Fritz Sandoz had kept there. There was a stool where Fritz sat while working, and an easy chair for his occasional visitor. The shop itself, where he sold clocks during the day, was in the front of the building down a little hall.

Peter Perkins put his derby on the desk and sat down in the easy chair, turning it so he could see what was going on in the big back room, where Fritz had housed his wonderful collection of fine old clocks.

His first feeling was of stunned grief. His next feeling was a determination that whoever was guilty should pay for his crime. In spite of Magrue's attitude, the big man was a conscientious detective. He just didn't like amateurs. But if Peter Perkins could offer some really good suggestion, Peter felt Magrue would listen.

One obvious place to look for possible clues was right there, in the office-workshop. The killer, after all, had spent some time there. He had had to rip open the drawers to find the hidden money—money Peter a dozen times had begged old Fritz to put in a bank.

Sitting quite still, Peter began to study the room. He studied the shelves which held clocks that had been repaired. He studied the big board full of little hooks from which hung watches of all kinds. He studied the desk, which also served as a workbench for old Fritz. Fritz's tools were still laid out on top of it. And a clock he had been working on—an electric clock, Peter noted with surprise—also stood on top of the desk. But Fritz was very neat. He always put away his tools when he stopped work. It was quite obvious, Peter realized, that Fritz had been interrupted in his work.

His gaze started to move onward. Then a realization of something queer brought it back again. The clock—there was something peculiar about the clock—something which disturbed him, and yet——

Then he realized what it was.

The clock was running backward!

Staring at it, watching the second hand spin in the wrong direction, watching the minute hand slowly reverse time itself, Peter Perkins felt a peculiar chill. It was just so—well, *unnatural*. Clocks always ran forward. But here was one running backward, and in the shop of Fritz Sandoz, whose great pride in life had been his ability to make clocks run forward and keep perfect time.

It was so strange that Peter Perkins felt that it must mean something, it *had* to mean something. But what?

That last is a very good question. Confidentially, the backward running clock does mean something, and something important. Perhaps you have already figured out what can be told from a clock running, not toward tomorrow, but toward yesterday? If not, don't forget the problem as we proceed.

Peter Perkins watched the minute hand move backward. Then he took a pad of paper from his pocket and a pencil. He made two small drawings and labeled them.

THE CORRECT TIME   THE TIME OF THE BACKWARD CLOCK

Then he rose and stepped toward the workbench-desk. He bent over and looked at the clock carefully. It was a very old electric clock—apparently one of the first ever made. A tag on it said *Mrs. Murphy,* which explained a lot. Mrs. Murphy lived across the street and often brought hot soup or other home-cooked food to old Fritz. For her, he would fix an electric clock, but not for anyone else. He hated them. The kind of clock he loved was the old-fashioned kind full of gears and springs.

A screwdriver lay beside the clock as if Fritz had just put it down. Peter had the distinct feeling that Fritz had actually been setting the clock when he had been interrupted. Suppose he had just set the clock to the correct time? Then he had looked up—perhaps to see an intruder with a gun. He had started the clock running. But he had started it *backward.* Why? Because he was so startled? Or had he done it with some calculated purpose? Fritz Sandoz was one man who knew all about clocks, what you could do with them, what——

"Perkins!"

The puzzle editor jumped. It was Detective Magrue, roaring in his ear. "I told you not to touch anything!"

"I haven't touched anything," Peter said. "But look—that clock is running backward."

Magrue gave it a glance.

"So what?" he said. "It's out of order and Fritz was going to fix it. Now go sit outside. The fingerprint men are going to work in here."

Peter did not argue. He went out into the big back room which held the scores of clocks that had been Fritz Sandoz' pride—"My family," he used to call them—and found a chair where he wouldn't be in the way. The room was humming with activity. The technical squad had arrived. A photographer took many pictures of the room and of poor

Fritz, lying at the foot of the big grandfather's clock where he had been struck down. Then the old clockmaker was covered and gently carried out. Fingerprint men were busy. Peter Perkins doubted that they would find anything. Detective Magrue was issuing orders, and other detectives and men in uniform came and went. At least they certainly were trying.

Peter Perkins was lost in his thoughts when one of the many clocks began to strike with silvery chimes. He waited for the others. Fritz had kept them in such perfect order, they all struck almost at once.

To his amazement, none of the other clocks struck. He looked for the clock that had struck. And then he gasped out loud.

A whole group of Fritz Sandoz' precious clocks were telling the wrong time! Not only that, but every one was telling a *different* wrong time.

It was simply incredible—as incredible as the clock that was running backward. Sudden excitement gripped Peter. The clocks that were telling the wrong time—were they telling more than that? Did they have a message to convey by their very wrongness?

With mounting eagerness, he studied the clocks. There were all kinds of clocks in the room, small and large, but directly opposite him was a row of tall grandfather clocks. One at the very end of the row was so huge and old that Fritz Sandoz had nicknamed it "Father Time." He had been lying at the foot of Father Time when Peter came into the room.

The first three clocks in the row told the correct time. Then came the terribly wrong clocks. Then came two more clocks telling the right time.

Peter took out his paper and pencil and sketched rapidly. When he had finished, the sketch looked as follows:

CORRECT CLOCKS   WRONG CLOCKS

WRONG CLOCKS (Continued)   CORRECT CLOCKS

He stared at the sketch, then slowly put it in his pocket. Those wrong clocks meant something, but for the life of him he didn't know what.

He sat back, thinking hard. As he sketched, he had become aware that all the clocks in the room had stopped except the twelve grandfather clocks. Which meant that Fritz Sandoz hadn't had time to wind them the previous night, so they had run down. He tried to picture to himself what had happened.

Fritz had locked up at six o'clock—he always did. Then he had fixed himself some supper in his living quarters and probably about seven he had gone into his workshop, where he usually stayed until midnight, unless a friend like Peter Perkins was present. Normally, at midnight exactly, he went in to wind his clocks.

Now it *looked* as if he had started to wind the clocks, had reached Father Time, and then had been struck down by someone who had slipped into the shop. So it *looked* as if he had been killed at midnight.

But Peter Perkins did not believe it.

He was sure Fritz had been busy in his workshop when the unknown had slipped in, startling him. Probably the thief had had a gun. He had threatened Fritz—and Fritz had started the electric clock running backward. Then the

unknown had made Fritz wind twelve of the clocks to make it look to the police as if the murder had happened at midnight. Fritz, knowing the man and knowing his life was in danger, had deliberately moved the hands of the wrong clocks while winding them. He had done it because he was trying desperately to leave a message for someone to read. Then he had been struck down brutally, and his killer had looted his desk for the hidden money and let himself out the back way, unseen.

And undoubtedly he had provided himself with a good alibi for midnight! But if that was true, how could they ever find out what time poor Fritz had really been killed?

Er—I just wanted to make a suggestion. If Peter's theory is correct—and I confess I rather approve of it—then the backward clock started running backward very shortly before the foul deed was committed. But how can you tell the right time from a clock running backward? Especially, how can you tell what time it was when the clock started running backward?

After long thought, Peter Perkins was positive he had a clear picture of just how the killer had left false clues to deceive them all. Now if he could convince Detective Magrue—

But Detective Dan Magrue was not interested in listening to theories by an amateur. Sometime later, when the activity had died down, he came out and dropped down onto a chair beside Peter Perkins.

"We'll find the killer," he said grimly. "Now this is how I figure it——"

"Detective Magrue———" Peter Perkins began.

"Don't interrupt me, Perkins," Magrue roared. "Do you realize you should be our number one suspect?"

"Me?" The puzzle editor was shocked.

"Yes, you. But I still can't see you killing anyone, so I'm looking elsewhere. However, the killer has to be someone who knew Fritz, who knew his habits, knew about the money. Someone who came here often enough to make an impression of the front door key and have a duplicate made. I hate to say it, but that means someone who lives and works right in this neighborhood."

"Yes." Peter nodded agreement.

"Now Fritz was killed last night, at midnight, as we can tell because he was winding his clocks. . . ."

"Detective Magrue," Peter began again, "that's what I want———"

"I said don't interrupt!" Magrue bellowed. "He was killed at midnight last night. Mrs. Murphy noticed he didn't open the store today. Tonight she brought him some hot soup, thinking he was sick, and when he didn't answer the bell she phoned us. That's how we discovered he'd been killed.

"Now, my men have been busy. I've got a list of names of five men in this very block who knew Fritz well—and they all are having money troubles. I'm pretty certain one of them did the job. Here's the list."

He showed Peter Perkins a penciled list, which Peter memorized. On it were the names:

> Jack Harrison, painter
> Thomas Fentriss, jeweler
> Bill Lawden, grocer
> Joseph Finchly, barber
> Bob Rogers, key maker

"My guess is it was either Rogers, who put a new lock on the door last month and could have kept an extra key, or Lawden, the grocer, who brought stuff here several times a week," Magrue told Peter. "But the others were all in and out, and could have made an impression of the key. Harrison painted the shop three months ago. Finchly trimmed Fritz's hair, and Fritz might have talked to him. Fentriss sent Fritz repair jobs that were too complicated for him. It could have been any of the five."

"He thought of them all as friends," Peter said, troubled.

"When it comes to money, friendship says good-by," Magrue said. "They all need money. For one reason and another. I'm going to question them personally, and the one who doesn't have an alibi for midnight last night— well, we've got our man!"

"But, Magrue," Peter tried again, "don't you see, the killer——"

"Perkins, stick to your puzzles and leave homicide to the experts," Magrue advised. "Now go on home."

Peter Perkins got his hat and his cane and left, his mind troubled. If only Magrue would listen! But he didn't try again to explain why he thought the murderer *wanted* the police to believe the murder had been committed at midnight, when actually it had been committed earlier. Magrue would just snort if Peter started talking about a clock that ran backward, and clocks that told the wrong time. If Peter could tell him what they meant . . . But he couldn't. Not yet.

He went home to his little apartment and, before he went to bed, spent an hour staring at the sketches he had made of the clocks. But no inspiration came to him.

He slept badly, because his mind was still occupied with the puzzle. Ordinarily Peter Perkins was very good at puzzles, but this one . . . Well, this one had to do with solving a real murder and somehow that made it different.

Er—I wonder if you spotted an important clue in the last few pages, or if it slipped right by you. It did? You will have to turn in your Sherlock Holmes deerstalker hat. But don't feel too badly. Peter Perkins missed it, too.

Next day in his tiny office at the newspaper Peter was unusually absent-minded. He opened letters from readers who sent him puzzles and jokes, scarcely reading them. Toward noon he telephoned Detective Magrue.

"Excuse me, Sergeant Magrue," he said, "but I wondered if you learned anything from questioning those five men you suspect killed Fritz."

"No." Magrue's tone was disgusted. "Every one of them had a perfect alibi for midnight. From ten o'clock on, in fact. Couldn't trip up one of them."

"Well, the fact is," Peter began, "I think——"

"Perkins, I'm busy," Magrue snapped, and hung up.

Peter hung up his own phone with a heavy heart. If he could only talk to someone—another puzzle fan who could give him a fresh viewpoint. He was too close to this, too anxious. Absently he opened a letter and looked at it.

It was a cryptogram—quite a good one. And it was signed, *Submitted by Daniel Magrue, Jr.*

Peter did a double take, Daniel Magrue, Junior! Why, that must be Detective Magrue's son! And he was a puzzle fan! The puzzle editor noted the street address, grabbed his derby and cane, and almost ran from his office. A taxi took him to the address in ten minutes. A tall, well-built boy was raking leaves in the front yard of the house. Peter hurried up the walk.

"Daniel Magrue?" he asked.

"Why, hello, Mr. Perkins," the boy said. "I recognize you from your picture in the paper. Did you get the cryptogram I sent you?"

"Yes, and I'm going to use it," Peter said. "But I'm here on something much more important."

He swiftly told Danny Magrue all about Fritz Sandoz and the wrong clocks.

"So you see," he finished, "I'm positive he was trying to leave a message when he changed the hands of those clocks." The boy nodded. "Now look, here's a sketch I made."

He showed Dan a sketch of the terribly wrong clocks:

WRONG CLOCKS

"It has to be a code of some sort," Peter said. "Fritz was an expert in codes and he probably expected *me* to be able to read this one because he knew I'd understand he was trying to leave us a message. But I can't see any way to crack a code with so few letters. Maybe you can see something I miss."

The boy frowned.

"I bet it is a code," he said. Absent-mindedly he sat down on the porch steps and Peter sat down beside him. They both squinted at the drawings of the mysteriously wrong clocks. At last Danny Magrue looked up.

"You know," he said, "these clock hands make me think of semaphore flags spelling out a message. I suppose that's really wild, but——"

"No!" Peter Perkins grabbed his arm. "Semaphore code! Fritz was in the Swiss Army Signal Corps when he was young. He must have known semaphore. But I don't. I've only studied secret codes."

"Well, gee, Mr. Perkins, I'm probably wrong," Danny Magrue said. "I'm a Scout and I know semaphore, and the position of these clock hands doesn't spell anything. A few odd letters, and some aren't even letters."

"But that's it, Danny!" Peter Perkins' eyes were bright with excitement now. "The clocks aren't telling the time Fritz set them at. They all have moved ahead since that happened. In order to read the message, we'd have to know when the hands were set, and figure out how they originally looked."

"Gosh, then I guess that's impossible," the boy sighed. "Mr. Sandoz had a good idea but he didn't realize how tough a message he was leaving us."

"But he did, Danny, he did." Peter Perkins almost shouted the words. "That's why he started the clock backward. What can you tell from a stopped clock?"

"That's easy. The correct time—twice a day."

"And what can you tell from a clock running backward, steadily backward, keeping absolutely correct time but always running toward the past?"

"I don't know." Danny Magrue stared at him. "What kind of a clock can run backward?"

"A very ancient electric clock, one of the first models. They had such simple motors they could be started spinning in either direction," Peter said. "Now look at this."

He showed the boy the sketch he had made of the electric clock the night before.

"So the correct time was six-forty," Danny Magrue mused. "But the backward clock said ten after twelve."

"And if the backward clock started backward at the cor-

THE CORRECT TIME   THE TIME OF THE
                     BACKWARD CLOCK

rect time, as I'm sure it did, every minute there's another
two minutes difference between it and the correct time,"
Peter stated.

"Mmm—yes." The boy was doing figuring in his head.
"But also the clocks are heading for the point where they'll
meet—which is the correct time and which they will hit
twice a day—at the rate of two minutes every minute."

"So if we move the hands of the backward clock *backward* some more, and of the forward clock *forward* some
more, the point where they both tell the same time is the
time the backward clock was started. Or, in other words,
the approximate time Fritz was killed!" Peter exclaimed.
"Oh, but wait a minute!"

"Something wrong, Mr. Perkins?" Danny asked.

"We've made a mistake," Peter Perkins groaned. "Since
one clock is going forward and one backward, the hands
will indicate the same time every six hours, or four times
every twenty-four hours. Two of those times will be the
moment at which they started, and two will be wrong by
six hours."

"Gosh." Danny sighed. "How can we ever figure out
which is which?"

Peter Perkins thought for a long minute, his face a
scowl of concentration. Then gradually the scowl cleared.

"I think I've got it," he said. "The suspects all have
alibis for after 10:00 P.M., and we're sure the crime was
committed after 6:00 P.M. That means the actual time of
the crime was between six and ten. Correct?"

"Yes, Mr. Perkins." Danny nodded. "That's absolutely correct."

"Then we figure the next time the hands will indicate the same time—if both clocks were still running, that is. If it is between six and ten, we'll know it's the time we're looking for. If it is between ten and four, we figure the alternate time, which will be just six hours later."

"That's it." Danny nodded after a moment. "It takes a little thinking but I see it now. It would be easier to work out if we had two clocks so we could actually turn the hands. Suppose we take my wrist watch and your wrist watch, and first set them at the times shown in your sketch, then move one forward and the other back until——"

"No, no, we could do that," Peter said, "but we can figure it in our heads even quicker. The backward clock is going backward from 12:10 A.M. The correct clock, on the other hand, is going forward from 6:40 P.M. The difference between them is—let me see—five hours and thirty minutes. Three hundred and thirty minutes. Since each is moving toward the other they will meet—or tell the same time— in precisely half that number of minutes. Half of three hundred and thirty is one hundred and sixty-five minutes. That in turn is two hours and forty-five minutes. Add two hours and forty-five minutes to 6:40 and we get—let's see— 9:25. Or subtract two hours and forty-five minutes from 12:10 and we likewise get—am I correct?—yes, we also get 9:25.

"In other words, the two clocks will tell the same time at 9:25, which is in the correct time period between six and ten. And so——"

"So Mr. Sandoz set the electric clock running backward at nine-twenty-five the night he was killed!" the boy cried.

"Precisely," Peter agreed. "At which time they looked

like this." And he made another sketch.

THE TIME THE
CRIMINAL APPEARED

THE TIME THE
BACKWARD CLOCK
STARTED BACKWARD

"Now we know what time Fritz must have changed the hands of the clocks telling the wrong time," Peter said. "Allow five minutes or so and it would have been about half-past nine when he started winding them and setting the hands wrong to spell out a message."

"And it was six-forty-five when you saw them and sketched them," Daniel Magrue said eagerly. "The difference between nine-thirty and six-forty-five is two hours and forty-five minutes. If we add just two hours and forty-five minutes to the time each of these wrong clocks says, we'll have the position at which Mr. Sandoz put the hands just before he was killed."

"Which will only take a moment, my boy!"

It took several moments. But presently Peter had another sketch:

THE POSITIONS AT WHICH
SANDOZ SET THE WRONG CLOCKS

Then he made a few more swift sketches, drawing under each a little figure holding semaphore flags in the position of the clock hands.

"There. Does that spell anything?"

"It sure does, Mr. Perkins!" Danny said. "In semaphore

code that's——"

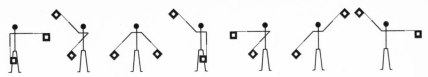

And with a pencil he drew a letter underneath each figure.

Peter stared at it and swallowed hard.

"Danny," he said, "that's the name of one of the suspects on your father's list. You've solved the mystery. But now you and I have to persuade your father we're right—and we have to persuade him to try something very unorthodox to capture the killer. Because, you see, no court would consider that poor Fritz's wonderful message provides a shred of legal evidence!"

Please do not feel left out of things. We have omitted the actual name of the killer only so you may have the pleasure of discovering it for yourself. I'm sure the matter of the clocks is clear to you now. I understood it completely after only four explanations. But you say you don't know semaphore code? Obviously a facet of your education has been sadly neglected. Nevertheless, you need not try to hide behind your ignorance. There's still another clue that Peter Perkins has quite overlooked, which needs no special knowledge at all to discover or apply. You may now go back and look for it if you wish a passing grade in this exercise in mystery. Or you may take the easy way and turn the page for the conclusion of our little conundrum

CONCLUSION

It was a strange group that met that evening in the big back room of Fritz Sandoz' Clock Hospital. First there was Detective Sergeant Magrue and half a dozen policemen. Then there were the five suspects, Jack Harrison, Bill Lawden, Joseph Finchly, Bob Rogers, and Thomas Fentriss. Keeping in the background was Danny Magrue, keyed up with excitement. Finally, there was Peter Perkins.

Peter, however, was unrecognizable. He wore a white robe and a huge turban and a very realistic false beard, all of which he had rented at a costume shop.

The meeting was his idea. After Danny Magrue had persuaded his father to listen to what he and Peter had figured out, Peter had told the detective that even though he was sure they knew the murderer's name, they had no proof. But they might be able to make him confess. After long argument, Magrue had agreed.

Disguised in his robes, Peter sat at a small table. The suspects sat in a semicircle facing him. The policemen guarded the door.

"Now, folks," Magrue said brusquely, "you're all gathered here voluntarily to help us solve Fritz Sandoz' killing, because you were his friends. I'll explain now what this is all about. Prince Ali here"—he pointed to the disguised puzzle editor—"is a mystic. Last night he received a spirit message from Fritz telling him that the clocks Fritz changed when he wound them the night he was killed would tell the name of his murderer. But when we got here, the clocks had all run down."

It was true. None of the clocks were ticking now. The police hadn't wound them.

"So," the detective continued, "Prince Ali is going to try to get in touch with Fritz Sandoz' spirit again tonight to learn who killed him."

The little group of five men stirred uneasily, but no one protested. Peter knew that the murderer remembered seeing Fritz change the hands of the clocks. He would be sweating now, wondering what that had meant.

"Now," said Magrue, "we're going to turn out the lights and let Prince Ali take over."

Peter Perkins closed his eyes as if meditating. Suddenly all the lights went out and the room was pitch black. He let a long minute go by before speaking. Then he made his voice deep and sepulchral.

"Fritz Sandoz," he said, "are you here? Is your spirit present?"

There was no sound but the hoarse breathing of the other men in the room. One of them coughed nervously.

"Fritz Sandoz," Peter said, "in life you had no voice. If you cannot speak, we understand. Show your presence some other way. Are you here?"

Very, very slowly, in the air over their heads, the word Y-E-S became visible, just a pale blue glow as if written on air.

Someone gave a strangled gasp. The word vanished.

"Is the one who killed you here?" Peter asked.

Again the word Y-E-S glowed like pale blue fire in the air.

Someone choked off an exclamation.

"Were you killed at midnight, two nights ago?"

This time the letters N-O appeared in mid-air.

"Were you killed at half-past nine?"

Y-E-S.

"Did you leave us a message, naming the criminal, by changing the hands of the clocks when he forced you to wind them?"

Y-E-S.

Someone was breathing very fast, and loudly.

"The clocks have stopped. Give us the name again in some other way."

A chair creaked as if someone in the darkness was getting ready to rise. For a long moment nothing more happened. Then, outlined on the glass face of one of the grandfather clocks, the letter F began to glow in a pale blue. It was followed by an I, then an N, then a C, an H, an L, a Y. Complete, it glowed in the dark. F-I-N-C-H-L-Y.

"No," someone shouted. "I didn't! I didn't!"

There was a scuffle of running feet, and a loud exclamation.

"Lights!" roared Magrue.

The lights came on. They saw the barber, Finchly, struggling with a policeman at the door.

"He was going to tell," the fat man cried out. "He found out I was making book on the horses in my back room, and selling bets on the numbers lottery. He was going to tell!"

"All right," Magrue said, "take him down to headquarters. I guess our little spirit séance is over."

Much later, Magrue clapped his son proudly on the shoulder and beamed at Peter Perkins.

"This boy is going to study criminology," he said. "But tell me, Peter, where did you ever get the idea for those blue lights and those words written on pieces of cheesecloth my men held up in the air while Danny turned an ultraviolet light on them?"

"Oh, that," Peter said. "Well, I just happened to be in

the House of Terror yesterday and I realized how frightening some luminous paint shining under ultraviolet light can be. I've had my hair cut by Finchly dozens of times and I know he is superstitious—he carries a rabbit's foot and never opens his shop on Friday the thirteenth. So I figured he might break down, with murder on his conscience."

"Which he did," Magrue said. "Peter, next time you have a theory I'm going to listen to it. Yes, sir, I'm going to listen."

And he slapped the puzzle editor on the back so hard that Peter's turban fell off. But Peter took it as a compliment.

ALFRED HITCHCOCK SPEAKING: *Next time you see a ghost, don't give it a thought—it's undoubtedly some left-over luminous paint. Unless, of course, you have something on your conscience. If you have any lingering doubts as to how Fritz Sandoz' ingenious message worked, get some clocks, preferably not your family's favorites, and follow the deductions made by Peter Perkins and Danny Magrue, actually turning the clock hands as suggested. I believe you will find it all works out neatly, simply and correctly. If it shouldn't, I will stoutly place all blame upon the shoulders of the proofreaders. . . . What about that clue I mentioned that Peter missed? Really, I hate to tell you. It's so simple that I . . . Well, if you insist. Go back and observe that exactly seven clocks were changed to give the code message. But there was only one suspect with seven letters in his name. So you could easily have picked out Finchly, couldn't you? And if you didn't think to count the wrong clocks—well, what's the title of our story? Exactly! The principal clue you needed was staring you in the face all along. But it's so easy to overlook the obvious, isn't it? Well, on to the next case!*

The Mystery of the Three Blind Mice

ALFRED HITCHCOCK SPEAKING: *Now that you are properly a-tingle with the excitement of the chase, I shall be brief in introducing the dark deeds that lie ahead. You are about to meet a three-hundred-pound millionaire who lives in a haunted castle, collecting stamps, but his real hobby is making people hate him. Some of you, I am told, take great pride in guessing the ending of mystery stories, movies, and television programs. I take a grave view of this trend. But if you do insist on guessing, I ringingly challenge you to guess all the twists and turns our story will take, as we unfold——*

The Mystery of the Three Blind Mice

— 1 —

FOREVER AFTER, Andy Adams would remember that tremendous, metallic voice screaming for help, bringing him out of a sound sleep with the blankets tangled around him and his heart thudding wildly.

"Help!" the voice shouted, echoing through Andy's bedroom. "Help!"

To Andy, still half asleep, it was like the voice of a giant in the room with him.

"He's shot me!" the voice cried, as Andy struggled to

wake up. "I suspect mice . . ."

Here the voice faltered. Then the unknown speaker tried again, each word seeming to be a terrible effort.

"I suspect mice . . ."

Then the voice gasped into silence, the final word sounding like m-y-y-y-s-s-s-s.

Andy's blindly groping hand found the chain of the bedside lamp. He looked around him at a totally strange room, noting the loud-speaker on the wall from which the voice had come, while his mind asked a crazy question.

How can anyone be shot by mice? he asked himself, trying to recall where he was and how he got there.

Then he remembered. . . .

"It's the only genuine haunted castle in North America," Porterfield Adams said.

His son Andy, almost as tall as he was but beanpole thin, looked around with awed interest. They were in a huge room, with a stone floor, stone walls, and a ceiling made of tremendous old beams. At one end a fire roared in a great fireplace.

Skins of animals covered the floor—zebras, lions, tigers, giraffes. Mounted heads of big game crowded the walls— water buffalo, wart hogs, tigers, lions, mountain goats, leopards and twenty more.

It was a room such as Andy had never dreamed of being in.

Up to nine o'clock that evening, the night before Thanksgiving, life had been perfectly normal. His mother being in Philadelphia with her ill sister, he and his father had been at home alone. They had been playing chess. Andy had won a game, lost a game, and was sure he could checkmate his father when the phone call came.

Porterfield Adams, who was a detective usually specializing in forgery and embezzlement cases and in authenticating old documents, wills and the like, had returned looking rueful.

"We're going on a case, son," he had said. "I tried to say no but got talked down. Pack a bag. We may be there several days."

Going on a case with his father! Andy was so excited he practically threw his pajamas, toothbrush, and extra shirt into a bag. Then had come an hour's drive through the rolling countryside of southern New England, ending at the strangest house Andy had ever seen. It was only two stories high, built like a square U, but it was made of enormous blocks of crude stone, and looked hundreds of years old. At each end was a kind of square tower. And, most surprising of all, it was completely surrounded by a water-filled moat, thirty feet wide, and could be reached only by a drawbridge. It looked just like old castles he had seen pictured in books.

The drawbridge had been lowered for them, and they had driven over the moat and parked in the space between the wings of the U-shaped building. Then a small man in a red coat and tight red trousers named Robin—a butler obviously—had shown them into the great living room.

And now his father was saying that it actually was a castle and haunted at that!

His survey of the room was interrupted. An enormously fat man with a totally bald head came gliding out of a doorway toward them, riding in an elaborate wheel chair driven by batteries and an electric motor. He came to a stop and, with tiny eyes set in a broad red face, gave Andy and his father a contemptuous stare.

"So you're the detective fella, eh?" he said, in strong English accents. "You don't look like a detective to me. And your name—Porterfield Adams! What sort of name is that for a proper detective?"

Andy felt hot with indignation, but his father remained calm. Taking out his pipe, the sturdily built detective looked at the enormous man in the wheel chair.

"Perhaps you'd like me better if I called myself Sherlock Holmes," he remarked. "And perhaps I'd like you better if you called yourself Sniffy Crumshaw."

For a moment Andy thought the big man would explode. He turned beet red and swelled up like an angry turkey gobbler. Then he let out a guffaw.

"You'll do," he said, as if satisfied. "But did you have to bring your brat with you?" And he turned on Andy a gaze of such intensity that Andy felt his skin crawl.

"My son," Porterfield Adams said, puffing pipe smoke. "You said your problem concerned stamps. Andy is a stamp collector. I brought him along as a consultant."

"Indeed?" And the fat man drawled the word like an insult. "Well, my lad, if you're such a bright lad, perhaps you can tell me what a killer is?"

It was such an unexpected question Andy blinked. But he thought he knew the answer.

"A killer, sir," he said, "is part of an obliterator."

A smile twitched at his father's lips. The fat man lifted bushy eyebrows.

"Now that may be," he said, "but suppose you tell me when a killer is *not* a part of an obliterator."

"When stamps are canceled," Andy answered, "the obliterator, which is usually known as the cancellation, consists of two parts. One is the postmark. The other part, which actually obliterates the stamp, is called the killer. If a sheet of stamps is canceled just so it can be sold at a reduced price to a collector, without being used for postage, there would be no postmark. Then the killer would be just a killer, I expect."

The fat man's expression did not change. But when he spoke after a long moment in which they could hear the fire crackling and the November wind howling through the branches of the many oak trees around the castle, his voice was civil.

"I am happy," he said, "to meet a fellow collector. Do you specialize?"

"In United States commemoratives," Andy told him.

"I," the fat man said, "specialize in rarities and errors of the most valuable type. I am happy to say that I own at least one, and sometimes as many as six, specimens of every important stamp known."

His lower lip thrust out as he said it, and Andy understood. The man was testing his knowledge.

"Excuse me," he said. "Maybe you are forgetting the one cent magenta of British Guiana, issue of 1856?"

"What about it?" The huge head lowered as if the man in the wheel chair was about to butt Andy.

"It is so rare that only one copy is known. Scott's catalogue values it at $50,000, but I've read the present owner won't sell. And I do know, sir, that you don't own it. So you can't own *every* important stamp known."

"No, you're right." The man's voice rumbled from deep in his chest. His face purpled again, and he seized a flexible rhinoceros-hide cane which lay on a nearby table and began to whack it furiously on the table top.

"I don't own it! I'll pay anything for it. A million dollars. And the idiot who owns it won't sell it. But I'll own it someday, somehow, or my name isn't Nigel Mayfair!"

And he whacked the table half a dozen times more before he stopped, panting, to glare at Porterfield Adams.

"I know what you're thinking, you detective Johnny," he growled. "You're thinking my name *isn't* Nigel Mayfair. Well, it isn't. But so help me, I shall own that one cent

Guiana stamp sooner or later. And then, sir, then I will be the world's foremost collector of stamp rarities!"

He got his breath and let it out with a roar.

"Henderson! Where are you? I want you!"

A tall, good-humored-appearing man in tweeds walked in from the next room.

"Right here, sir," he said.

"Henderson," Nigel Mayfair grunted, "this is Adams, the detective fella you persuaded me to send for. Adams, Bert Henderson, a solicitor—no, it's lawyer in this country—one of my legal Johnnies."

They shook hands. Then the sandy-haired lawyer shook Andy's hand firmly.

"Glad you could both come," he said. "Do you want to give Mr. Adams the details now, sir."

"No, blast it, not yet. First I want him to meet the rest of the scavenging jackals who live by picking the flesh from my bones. Where's Pardo?"

"Coming now, sir." A burly man with broad shoulders, dressed expensively, came walking down a flight of carpeted stone stairs from the second floor.

"Pardo!" Nigel Mayfair roared. "This is Adams, the detective. With his help I'm going to put somebody in this house behind bars. That is, if I don't do something worse to 'em."

"Yes, sir," Pardo said; his accent also was English.

"Pardo is my bruiser, my bodyguard and chauffeur," Mr. Mayfair said. "But that doesn't mean he may not be the jackal who has had the nerve to rob me. . . . Pardo! Where's my sister-in-law and that human excuse of a stepson who's been inflicted on me for my sins?"

"They will be down in a moment, sir," Pardo said. His tone was that of a trained servant, but the look he gave Mr. Mayfair was ugly with hate. "They are dressing to go to the party which Mr. Howard Muyskens is giving this evening to celebrate the fact that tomorrow is Thanksgiving. They wish me to drive them. Shall I do so, sir, or shall I call them a taxi?"

"Drive 'em, drive 'em," the fat man roared. "What do I care how they get to the house of that unprincipled thief? The mere fact they defy me and go speaks for itself. Ah, here they are."

He turned his chair, and Andy and his father saw a handsome woman, in evening dress and expensive furs, coming down the stairs. A young man in a tuxedo, his pale face sulky, was at her side. They reached the main floor and paused. Nigel Mayfair glowered at them.

"So you're going," he said. "After I told you I think he's conniving at having me robbed. After I told you he's no better than a thief and a blackguard and a swindler."

The woman shrugged.

"My dear Nigel, you're just ridiculous," she said. "Howard is a fine man. You're merely jealous of him because he has shot specimens of big game larger than you ever did, and is a much better judge of stamps than you."

"Be careful you don't drive me too far, Mollie," Nigel Mayfair growled. "Just because I was married to your sister doesn't allow you to speak to me as you choose."

"This is America," his sister-in-law said. "And you are no longer a petty king ruling over a frightened kingdom. I wasn't going to tell you yet, but I will. I'll be leaving this ridiculous castle for good, soon. Howard Muyskens and I are going to be married."

Nigel Mayfair drew a deep breath. Andy waited for an explosion—but it did not come. In the silence Reggie, the stepson, spoke.

"And I'll go with my aunt," he said. "Tomorrow, however, I have a date to join a sports car rally. Just wanted you to know. Good night, dear stepfather. Pleasant nightmares."

"Tomorrow one of you may be in jail!" the fat man roared.

Without turning they walked out of the room, followed by Pardo, the chauffeur.

"So she's going to marry Muyskens, eh?" Nigel Mayfair growled, half to himself. He looked at the lawyer, Henderson. "Maybe she's the one. Maybe that's her reward for stealing my stamps from me? Or maybe Reggie is doing it for her—he's devoted to her. They both hate me. Just like everybody in this house hates me.

"You hear that?" he demanded of Porterfield Adams. "Everybody who meets me hates me. You'll come to hate me, too, you'll see."

Andy thought his father was going to laugh, the fat man sounded so full of self-pity. But though his lips twitched, the detective's expression never changed.

"I imagine you make it easy for them," he commented.

Nigel Mayfair gave him a sour look.

"No impertinence, my man!" he snapped. "You're just a hired hand here to do a job, so don't get above yourself."

"Andy." His father turned to him. "On second thought I've decided not to take Mr. Mayfair's case, whatever it is. Let's get the car and return home."

"No!" the fat man's roar filled the room. "Confound it, you New Englanders are so touchy. Have been ever since that Boston Tea Party business and that was almost two hundred years ago. Come in to my private study and let's get down to brass tacks. . . . And," he added, as Porterfield Adams hesitated, "I expect you to bill me for the services of your consultant, too."

Andy looked at his father so excitedly that Porterfield Adams gave a reluctant laugh.

Maybe, Andy was thinking, I really will be able to help. Until now, his father's work had always seemed mysterious to him, but if this case involved stamps . . .

"All right," the detective said. "Lead the way."

"Henderson, I'll call you when I need you." The fat man turned the wheel chair, and it rolled toward a doorway. Henderson nodded cheerfully to Andy and his father and settled down on a sofa covered in leopard skin.

"If he starts yelling too much, I'll come in," he half whispered. "Mr. Mayfair sometimes gets a bit—well, excited."

— 2 —

Andy, following his father, found himself in a much smaller room. It too, however, seemed to have walls of crude stone, covered with animal skins. Several suits of armor on stands stood along the floor, and on the walls were just six mounted big game heads—a lion, a tiger, a mountain goat, a black leopard, a water buffalo and a grizzly bear. Andy had seen living animals of these species in zoos, but these heads must have come from specimens that were absolute giants. Even mounted, they seemed tremendously alive, as if about to leap upon them all and rend and tear them to bits.

"Close the door," Nigel Mayfair directed, and Andy did so. The fat man waved his rhinoceros-hide cane toward two chairs, and they sat down. Porterfield Adams was puffing calmly on his pipe, but Andy was almost quivering inside with excitement, though he tried hard to imitate his father and seem calm.

"This cane," said the fat man in the wheel chair, "came from the skin of a rhino I shot myself. Those heads on the wall—shot 'em all myself. They're the largest ever taken, I don't care what that blackguard Howard Muyskens says. If he has larger, he got 'em by a trick—natives trapped 'em or something."

On the point of getting into a fury, he calmed himself.

"Going to talk about myself for a moment," he said. "Want you to understand me. Important to understand the kind of man you're dealing with, eh, detective fella?"

Andy's father nodded. "It helps," he said.

Andy listened, eyes and ears both wide open.

"Well," said Nigel Mayfair, "I'm a collector, see. Started life in a London slum. Not nice. Then or now. Sharpens a lad's wits, though." He bared his teeth in what Andy supposed was a grin.

"That's when I was named Sniffy Crumshaw. Had a cold all the time. Runny nose. Those days I collected bottles. Cleaned 'em and sold 'em for half a cent each. When I got enough money, I went to South Africa. Got a job with a big diamond-mining company. Figured out a brand-new way to smuggle diamonds out of the mines, past the guards. I was a millionaire before I was twenty-one. Then I collected my name. Nigel Mayfair. More aristocratic sounding."

His eyes bored into theirs.

"Yes, sir. When I was Nigel Mayfair, gentleman millionaire, I started collecting money. Collected plenty of it. When a chap collects anything—money or anything else—sometimes he forgets about the nice points of the law, eh?" And he bared his teeth in another sharklike grin.

"When I had enough money, I started collecting big game. Real thrill in those days, shooting big game. Married a British aristocrat—widow of a duke. We had a grand time. But then a tiger killed her in India and I was saddled with her pasty-faced son Reggie and her sister, Mollie Rainier, both of whom you saw. They live off me and look down on me 'cause I was born in a slum and they were born in a manor house.

"Well, I caught a tropical illness. Made an invalid out of me. So I moved here, to New England. Doctor fellas said the climate would do me good. To show Reggie and Mollie what money can do, I went out and bought myself a whole castle—this one. Castle Cragie, it was called. It came complete with ghost, though he doesn't show himself these days —maybe he didn't like crossing the Atlantic."

The fat man's eyes gleamed with satisfaction now, and his voice had become almost a purr.

"Yes, I bought a castle—not big, but real. And old. Stood on the Scotland-England border for four hundred years. Changed hands a dozen times. Blood ran deep on these floors more than once in the days when the Scots and the British were constantly at war."

He said it so happily that Andy glanced down and moved his feet, almost as if expecting to see a pool of blood. His father winked at him, meaning, *Let him enjoy himself talking.* His father had often told him that the more a man talked, the more you could tell about his character, his personality, and even how he would be apt to think.

"So I brought every stone here and had it put up the way it was. Castle Cragie had a drawbridge. I kept the drawbridge and put a real moat around it. Of course I added electricity, an elevator, things like that; but just the same, I'm the only man in North America who lives in a genuine haunted castle with a moat around it. That's a satisfaction, knowing you have something no one else has. Believe me it is, lad." And he spoke now to Andy.

"As a collector, you know how much fun it is to have a rare stamp your friends don't have. Well, I have things no other man has. And now that I'm an invalid, and have to collect stamps, I'm going to have stamps nobody else has! The most, the best, and the rarest!"

And to punctuate his statement, he whacked the rhinoceros-hide cane loudly against the floor.

"I think we understand," Porterfield Adams said now, putting his pipe away. "But that still doesn't tell me—us— anything about your problem." Andy felt a little thrill of pride when his father added that "us."

"So it doesn't. Well, step to the wall." Nigel Mayfair used the whip to point. "Pull back that zebra skin."

The detective rose and did so. Behind the zebra skin, Andy was startled to see a great steel vault with a man-sized square door, the bottom flush with the floor. It seemed to Andy to have a very elaborate combination lock.

"Open it," the fat man growled. "I unlocked it when you came. And snap that light switch beside the door."

Porterfield Adams tugged at the handle and the vault door swung open. Behind it was a strongroom, six feet wide by eight feet long and six feet high. The walls were of steel. In it were a small desk and a chair, and shelving, hung low, which held dozens of large, leather-bound books.

"My treasure chest. I can roll my chair right into it," Nigel Mayfair said. "More'n a million dollars' worth of stamps in there. Fireproof. Burglar proof. Even if an army with cutting torches tried to burn their way in, they'd be sorry." He gave an ugly chuckle. "Poison gas," he said. "It would flood the vault and this room, too.

"What's more," he told the detective, "the combination is a six-letter word nobody on heaven or earth knows but me. Six letters. Not a chance in a million any thief could stumble on the right combo. But"—and he began to pound the rhinoceros-hide cane violently on the floor— "some beggar has got in. Somebody in this house has got into my vault and stole some of my most precious little beauties!"

"Calm yourself, sir!" Andy's father said sharply. "I understand your feelings, but getting excited doesn't help me get the facts."

"No, of course not." With an effort, the enormous man in the wheel chair composed himself. "But you don't understand, detective fella. I mean, they've robbed *me*, Nigel Mayfair! And taken some of my sweetest rare stamps! To steal from a collector is to steal more than money, sir!"

Porterfield Adams waited. After a moment, Mr. Mayfair began again.

"All right," he said. "It's only half a dozen stamps. Maybe worth twenty, thirty thousand dollars. But somebody in this house stole 'em. Maybe my sister-in-law. Maybe Reggie. Maybe Pardo, maybe Henderson. Maybe Robin. Maybe Frenchy the chef—no, he just lives to cook. Count him out. But somebody in this house. And I think they sold them to that confounded Muyskens, who lives the next house to me, only house anywhere near. Or if Mollie did it, maybe she made him a present of 'em. For love. Bah!"

He made an ugly sound in his throat and fixed his eyes on Andy.

"I don't go in there to look at my treasures every day," he said. "Sometimes not for weeks. I might not have discovered the theft for a long time—maybe not until the cheeky thief took everything I own! Only, a little while ago, a couple of chaps reported they had some of the new United States Dag Hammarskjöld commemorative four-cent stamps with errors in them—you know what I mean, eh?" he asked Andy.

"Yes, sir." Andy did know. "Several men reported having the Dag Hammarskjöld errors. One, out in the Middle West, had used some for postage. Another one, here in the East, had a complete sheet. He valued it highly."

"He did indeed," Nigel Mayfair said. "But I made him an offer to double any other bid, and I'd have gotten it, too. Then I would have had a complete sheet of the first important error in United States stamps since the discovery of a sheet of twenty-four-cent airmail stamps with the airplane in the center inverted, way back in 1918. And you know what happened?" He raised his voice now to a roar. "You know what happened?"

Andy thought he knew what Mr. Mayfair was leading up to. But the fat man did not wait for any answer.

"That postmaster general in Washington!" he shouted, his face livid and the limber hide cane swishing down to smack on the floor with almost every word. "He decided to reprint millions more just like the original errors so everybody could have one. Said stamp collecting wasn't a lottery. Why, the brass-bound nerve of the fella. He robbed me of the chance to have that whole sheet of original errors. Worth a genuine fortune someday! Now, I wouldn't have 'em in the house!

"But"—and he was still roaring at the top of his voice, with the veins in his temples standing out in a way that alarmed Andy—"it made me look at my book of rarities and errors. And I found I'd been robbed. And I began to get mad. I wanted someone's hide. Someone's got to be punished, got to pay, got to suffer——"

He was actually screaming now. But just as Andy's father was about to go to him the door burst open and Pardo rushed in, followed by Henderson, and Robin, who looked white and frightened.

"I'll take over, sir," Pardo said, and seized the fat man. As Mr. Mayfair opened his mouth to roar his anger, Pardo put a small bottle to his lips.

"That will help him, Mr. Adams," Henderson said. "It's for his heart and nerves. This stamp business has really upset him—I mean first the losing out on the Dag Hammarskjöld errors, then finding he'd been robbed."

Nigel Mayfair was returning to normal. He still breathed

heavily, but his face turned from purple back to its normal reddish tinge.

"Thanks, Pardo," he said. "You delivered the lady and dear Reginald to my esteemed neighbor's party, eh?"

"Yes, sir," Pardo said. "It appears to be a large, noisy American type party. Mr. Muyskens will bring them back. I shall work on the car if you do not require me. The carburetor needs adjusting."

"After you get me into bed," Mr. Mayfair said. "I'm going to sit up and write a letter to the President, telling him what I think of the postmaster general. I'll singe the paper, blast me. Adams!"

"Yes?"

"We'll finish our chat in the morning. Ask Robin for anything you want. Pardo, take me upstairs."

"Yes, sir." The big man stepped to the far wall. He pressed a button. What to Andy had looked like rock proved to be a cunningly painted door, which slid back to reveal a small elevator. Nigel Mayfair guided his electric wheel chair into the elevator without looking back.

"Good night, gentlemen," Pardo said, and closed the door. Then he and Nigel Mayfair were gone.

Once they were out of sight, Andy suddenly realized he had been almost too tense to breathe. Mr. Mayfair's rage had been so violent that the boy felt as if he had been through some kind of storm.

The lawyer, Henderson, stepped across to the open stamp vault, closed it and spun the combination. Then he clicked the switch that controlled the light inside the vault.

"He really was upset!" he remarked. "Going off and leaving his treasure chest open. Please witness I closed and locked it. Believe me, he suspects me as much as anyone else in this ridiculous castle."

He cocked an eyebrow at Andy.

"What do you think of Mr. Nigel Mayfair?" he asked.

"I don't like him!" Andy said. "He practically boasted that all his life he's lied and cheated and stolen to get what he wanted."

"If not much worse," Henderson said.

"At any rate," Porterfield Adams remarked, "things should be quiet now. You can give me a few facts, if you don't mind, Mr. Henderson."

"Glad to."

"And you, son, ought to get to bed now." He smiled at Andy. "I'll be along soon. Nothing much more can happen tonight, I'd say."

He was wrong. Very wrong. But they would not know that for almost an hour.

I feel I have been most unobtrusive, remaining silent for so long. So, as Andy starts for bed, perhaps you'll let me sum up a few points that have occurred to me. First, the character of Mr. Nigel Mayfair, born Sniffy Crumshaw. Obviously he can't bear to think that anyone can own anything he can't own. A subtle point, perhaps, yet keep it in mind. It will loom important at a later moment!

Next, you who are stamp collectors will easily have deduced the date of this case—the night before Thanksgiving, 1962. The reference to the Dag Hammarskjöld four-cent commemorative errors, which were discovered in the fall of that year, places the time for us. November is apt to be a chilly, windy month in southern New England. I hope you noted that the wind was blowing strongly that night. Also notice that most of the trees on the estate were oaks. What, you may ask, is special about oak trees? Well, oak wood makes good furniture. Oak trees have acorns. They keep their dead leaves until late in the fall, not dropping them as other trees do. Oak bark can be used in tanning. Is this any help?

— 3 —

Robin, the butler, led Andy up the broad stairs to the second floor, to a room a short way down a wide hall. It was a huge room, with furniture that looked very old, and two immense beds with carved bedposts. On one of them lay Andy's pajamas. His father's lay on the other bed.

"Tonight, Master Andrew," the butler said, "you will sleep in a bed in which kings have slept. Not English kings, but kings for all that. Every stick of furniture Mr. Mayfair owns was bought from various European royal households. Where he walks, kings walked. Where he sits, kings sat. He—ah—enjoys the thought."

It gave Andy a queer feeling to think he was going to sleep in a bed that had once been occupied by a king, or maybe kings.

He walked over to the windows and looked out. He could see one wing of the building, looming large and dark at his left. A light on the second floor was on. To his right he could make out the east wing of Castle Cragie. A whole row of lights were on.

The wind was whipping and lashing the oak trees that stood on the grounds beyond the moat, and he could see a positive blaze of lights appearing and disappearing off to his left, just beyond the end of the west wing, but quite a distance away.

"What's that light, Robin?" he asked, not sure how one talked to a butler.

"The light in Mr. Henderson's room, sir. He has the last room in the west wing. Mr. Mayfair occupies the entire east wing himself."

"No, I mean off there in the distance."

"Oh, that. That is Mr. Howard Muyskens' residence, where the party is. Mr. Muyskens and Mr. Mayfair were once friends and indeed, partners, but I fear they are enemies now. Would you like a hot bath, sir?"

Andy decided he would, especially when he saw that the room had a private bath with a tub almost big enough to swim in, made of solid pink marble with real gold fixtures.

"What temperature do you prefer, Master Andrew?" Robin asked, as he turned on the water. Andy had never thought of taking the temperature of a bath. It was either too hot, or too cold, or just right. But he tried to be nonchalant.

"Whatever you think, Robin," he said, and couldn't help feeling a little embarrassed at having a grown man help him take a bath. "Tell me," he asked, as Robin turned on the taps, "did Mr. Mayfair shoot all those animals downstairs?"

"Oh, no, sir." The little man got an immense towel out of a cabinet and folded it for use.

"Miss Rainier, his sister-in-law, shot some. His stepson Reginald shot some. One or two were shot by Pardo, and I have the honor to be represented by a small but rare species of cheetah."

"Then everybody in the house is a big-game hunter?" Andy asked in surprise.

"Everybody but cook, sir. Even Mr. Henderson has done a bit of shooting. Only deer, however."

Andy hoped he wasn't being too nosy, but a detective had to ask questions and get information, didn't he? And he might learn something that would help his father.

"Robin," he asked, "does everybody really hate Mr. Mayfair?"

The butler cleared his throat.

"Mr. Mayfair makes himself easy to dislike, sir," he said.

"Do you hate him? Does Pardo hate him? Everybody?"

"If Mr. Mayfair had not already stated the fact," the

little man said with dignity, "I would not speak of it. But it is true. We all hate him completely. Even Miss Rainier and Mr. Reginald."

"Gosh, then, why do you stay around?" Andy burst out. "This is America, not—not someplace else."

"It is not that simple, Master Andrew. Sometimes one makes—shall we say, a misstep? It is very easy, especially when one is desperate. Mr. Mayfair has certain papers in a small steel box in his vault which keep us loyal and faithful to him."

"You mean he blackmails you?"

"I do not like that word, Master Andrew."

"Even Mr. Henderson?" Andy asked. Robin nodded. "And Miss Rainier? And Reggie?"

"Miss Rainier and Mr. Reginald," Robin said, "are quite penniless and in debt. Mr. Mayfair supports them but will not let them leave. Meanwhile he withholds a small estate his wife left them, which would enable them to be independent. Now, sir, would you care to have me return to towel you when you finish your bath? Or shall I remain to assist in scrubbing your back?"

"Gosh, no!" Andy burst out. "I can bathe myself. Uh— that will be all," he finished, using a line he had heard in a movie.

"Very good, sir. Good night."

Robin seemed to glide out, and Andy gave a little sigh of relief. He didn't think he would like having a servant around all the time.

Still, the bath in the huge tub with the gold fixtures was rather fun, and he prolonged it because he felt sure he would never encounter such luxury again. When he finally tumbled into one of the two big beds, he was asleep almost before he could turn out the light.

And it was out of a sound sleep that the giant voice

awakened him, echoing through the room.

"Help!" the voice cried. "Help!"

Andy shot bolt upright in bed, fighting to get loose from the blankets, trying to get his eyes open.

"He's shot me!" the voice screamed, so metallic and distorted that Andy couldn't recognize it. "I suspect mice . . ."

Then the voice faltered before the unknown speaker tried again, this time the words coming slowly, as if with great effort.

"I suspect mice . . ."

The voice gasped into silence, so that the last word was long drawn out, sounding like m-y-y-y-s-s-s-s.

Andy's blindly groping hand found the chain of the bedside lamp. He looked around at the strange room, trying to recall where he was and how he got there.

Then he remembered and leaped out of bed. His father's bed had not been touched. He ran to the door, flung it open and dashed into the hall. Down the hall he saw his father disappear through a door, and he raced after him.

"Dad!" he called. "Dad!"

Apparently his father did not hear him. The door closed. But when Andy reached it, he wrenched it open and darted inside. He found himself in a tremendous room with many windows, hung with rare old tapestries. His father was standing beside a great four-poster bed where Mr. Nigel Mayfair lay slumped on his side, gasping for breath, eyes shut, one hand still beside the button of the communicator into which he had been shouting, and which apparently connected with all the other rooms in the house. The bed reading lamp was on and some papers were scattered on the pillow.

Porterfield Adams turned.

"Andy!" he said. "Someone's shot Mayfair. Sitting up in bed with the light on, he was a perfect target. He may be dying. We have to get a doctor."

He bent over the communicator, which had enabled Mr. Mayfair to speak to all parts of the house.

"Robin! Pardo!" he shouted. "Get here at once!"

Then he straightened. His gaze went to the window. Andy's followed. In the center window, he saw three bullet holes, neat round punctures surrounded by radiating cracks. Drawn by a strange fascination, Andy walked toward the window. He looked out, through one of the bullet holes, and saw again, directly in his line of vision, the lights of the Muyskens residence, blinking and winking at him.

"Dad," he began, turning. But before he could speak, Pardo rushed into the room, his hands black with grease. Behind him came Robin, tugging on his red jacket, and immediately after Robin was Mr. Henderson, still pulling a robe over his pajamas and wearing one bedroom slipper.

Porterfield Adams issued crisp orders.

"Robin!" he said. "Phone Mr. Mayfair's doctor. Tell him to get here at once, and have the nearest hospital send a fully equipped ambulance to meet him. Pardo, do anything you can for Mr. Mayfair. He's still alive, but just barely. Henderson, check the grounds to see if anyone outside could have fired those shots. I'll phone the State Police. . . . Oh, and Andy—go back to bed!"

Andy had been about to tell him he knew where the shots had come from. But when his father used that tone, it was no time for talk.

"Yes, sir," he said and started for his room.

It was only after he was in bed that he realized what kind of mice had tried to kill Mr. Mayfair.

Seriously wounded, Mr. Mayfair had tried to gasp into the house communicator the name of the person he suspected. He had been trying to say, "I suspect Muyskens." Only, he had just been able to get out the *mice* sound.

And then another idea came to Andy. Maybe he had been trying to say, "*My s*ister-in-law." That started with the *mice* sound, too. Or even, "*My s*tepson." Another *mice*.

Three mice, Andy thought, yawning, and any of them might have shot Mr. Mayfair. His thoughts began to spin in queer circles. . . . *Muyskens . . . my sister-in-law . . . my stepson . . . three mice and we're the blind ones because we don't know which of them did it . . . the mystery of the three blind mice . . .*

Finally, in spite of all the excitement of the evening—or perhaps because of it—he was asleep.

Permit me to interrupt long enough to inquire if you have spotted a certain clue which—while it does not actually prove anyone guilty—certainly does suggest the innocence of one or more of our suspects. And if we can eliminate enough suspects, whoever is left will have to be It. If you missed the clue, it will do no harm to reread the last few pages. At the very least it will give you practice in reading and make the book last longer. Indeed, it might help to study the whole story from the beginning, in the light of the events just recounted. I wasn't going to tell you, but carried away by a spirit of generosity, I shall reveal that an extremely suggestive clue made a brief appearance early in our drama and will not be seen again. Having said that much, my lips are sealed.

— 4 —

When Andy woke, it was broad daylight. His father's bed had been slept in, but his father was missing. Andy's wrist watch said 9:30. Why, they might have solved the whole case of the stolen stamps and the shooting of Mr.

Mayfair already for all he knew.

He washed, brushed his teeth, slid like an eel into his clothes, and dashed out of the room. In the hall, he paused. Down at the end, the door to Mr. Mayfair's room was open.

Drawn irresistibly, he walked quietly toward it. When he reached it, he saw the room was empty. Mr. Mayfair had been taken away, probably to a hospital. If the door had been closed, he wouldn't have gone in, but as it was wide open, he now walked in boldly.

In the carved wood of the headboard was a bullet hole— apparently one bullet had missed, probably when Mr. Mayfair rolled over to shout for help into the communicator beside the bed.

Someone had taped a black string beside the bullet hole and the string led straight to the window. Eagerly Andy went to the window and saw that the string was taped there just beside the third bullet hole. He could tell it was the third bullet hole quite easily.

The first bullet, cutting a clean hole through the glass, had left cracks radiating out to the edges of the pane. The second bullet had left cracks which stopped when they met the cracks made by the first bullet. The third bullet's cracks stopped even sooner—when they met the cracks made by the second bullet.

Andy could see what the idea was. By lining up the two holes made by the same bullet, someone had been deter- mining the exact line of flight of the bullet!

Andy bent over and sighted along the string. His gaze went through the hole in the glass and, just as he had ex- pected, it ended directly at the terrace on the side of the large brick and timber house several hundred yards away, and up a slight rise. The home of Mr. Howard Muyskens.

Andy stood and looked over the whole landscape with

great care.

The wind of the night before had died down. He could see a section of the thirty-foot moat which surrounded Castle Cragie. The water was glittering in the sunlight. Beyond it was a line of oak trees, spaced evenly apart, then a stone wall, then three hundred yards farther, the Muyskens residence.

And the bullet had come directly between two oak trees, where a space of six feet or more gave a clear view, straight into Mr. Mayfair's room.

In its flight, it had cleared the end of the west wing of Castle Cragie by about five or six feet. Andy transferred his gaze to the west wing, to see if he could be wrong, if by any chance the shot could have been fired from there.

The very end window, in Mr. Henderson's room, was open a few inches, but the angle was all wrong. The shot couldn't have been fired there. Maybe if there was a ledge—but there wasn't any ledge. No, the shot could not have been fired from the house, nor from anywhere on the grounds that he could see—the paved terrace, the green lawn, the little garden below him, between the building and the moat.

Then Andy's heart leaped with excitement. Just beyond the west wing he could see the lower section of a ladder leaning against the building. It obviously leaned against the end of the west wing. He could see easily enough that no one could have stood on top of it to fire the shot, because they would have been around the corner of the building and would not even have been able to see Mr. Mayfair's window. But he had another idea, such a startling idea that he wondered if his father had thought of it. Why, if he was right, it could change the whole picture of the case!

He ran out pell-mell to find his father. Dashing down

the stairs, he almost knocked little Robin down.

"Robin," he cried as he steadied the butler, "do you know where my father is?"

"In the west library, sir." Robin pointed. "He's making notes, I believe."

"And has he solved the case yet?"

"I do not believe so." Robin did not seem the least bit unhappy as he said it. "The State Police are here and have questioned us all. However, it is my impression they are totally baffled!"

"Thanks, Robin!" Andy headed for the door the butler had indicated.

But, passing another door that was partly open, he stopped.

Inside, a police officer he knew, Lieutenant Dick Fields of the nearest State Police barracks, was questioning a tall, hook-nosed man with a shock of black hair. That must be Howard Muyskens, he thought.

Andy didn't mean to eavesdrop, but after all, this was a detective case and he was there as an official consultant, wasn't he? Besides, the door was open. He bent over, just beyond the door, and tied and retied his shoelace while he listened.

"Now, Mr. Muyskens"—Lieutenant Fields' voice sounded weary—"here is a rifle which my men fished out of the moat. It is a Belgian hunting rifle, with a telescopic sight, and I imagine it is probably accurate up to 500 yards."

"A thousand yards," Muyskens said cheerfully. "Wonderful sight, that. Makes the target look ten feet away. Yes, it's my rifle. I kept it in my trophy room along with some others. It must have been stolen from there."

"Have you any idea when?"

"Not the foggiest. That room is at the side of the house. Sometimes I don't enter it for days. Could have been stolen last night, or maybe a couple of days ago. Hmm. I suppose whoever used it threw it into the moat because he was afraid to try to return it with my party going on. Someone might have wandered in."

"You didn't, perhaps, slip away from your party and use this gun yourself?" the Lieutenant asked.

"To shoot old Mayfair? Hardly sporting, Lieutenant, to shoot a man sitting up in bed like that. No, I didn't shoot him. I was with my guests all evening, as you have already learned by asking."

"But you are enemies?"

"Wrong. He may hate me, but I rather admire him. He's so incredible. Actually he's angry because I'm going to marry Miss Rainier. In fact, I settled here to be near her."

"And you haven't been buying any of the stamps stolen from him?"

"Stamps he *says* were stolen. The answer is no."

"Thank you." Lieutenant Fields sighed. "Miss Rainier?"

"Yes, Lieutenant?" Andy heard the voice of the handsome woman he had seen leaving the night before.

"Have you anything to add to your statement of last night?"

"Nothing. I did not shoot Nigel. I admit I could have, and I have often been strongly tempted to kill him. But I didn't. I was with the other guests the whole time."

"But you could have shot him at 300 yards with that telescopic hunting rifle?"

"Easily, my dear lieutenant, easily. I'll be glad to demonstrate my ability if you desire."

"That won't be necessary. Now, Mr. Reginald Whitford."

"Aren't we just wasting time, old man," Andy heard Reggie's languid voice say. "I didn't shoot the old boy either. But I could have, and maybe I would have if I'd thought of it. My alibi is the same—I was with the other

guests. Now be a good fellow and let me have some breakfast? I have a sports car rally to attend this afternoon."

As it seemed the questioning would be coming to an end,
Andy hastily headed for the west library, where he found
his father seated at a desk, bending over a sheet of paper.

"Dad!" he said excitedly. "Is Mr. Mayfair . . . well, is
he . . . ?"

"He's at the hospital, unconscious," his father said, looking up. "It's touch and go. If he lives, it may be days
before he can talk."

"And you haven't any idea what mouse shot him?" Andy
blushed, realizing his slip of the tongue, but his father
chuckled.

"That *mice* thing has been driving me and the police a
bit daffy, too, son," he said. "Oh, here's Lieutenant Fields.
Learn anything more, Dick?"

"Not a thing." The youngish, trimly erect State Trooper
sat down at the desk. At that moment Robin came in with
a tray, which held two cups of coffee, a glass of milk, two
soft boiled eggs and a pile of toast. He put the coffee
in front of the men and the food before Andy.

"I took the liberty, Master Andrew," he said. Andy, suddenly ravenous, was glad he had. He began to eat as the
two men talked.

"We've got to make an arrest fast, Porter," Dick Fields
said, sipping his coffee. "Otherwise think of the stories in
the papers! A real castle—a moat and a drawbridge—a
locked vault—a millionaire stamp collector—a shot out of
the night. The victim tries to name the one he suspects and
can only say *mice!* Wow! The headlines!"

"That vault." Porterfield Adams' brow wrinkled. "I wish
we could get it open. Until we do, we don't know what's
been stolen. Also, there might be a clue inside."

"Robin told me Mr. Mayfair keeps papers there that

would cause trouble for the people who work for him!" Andy burst in. "He blackmails them into being loyal to him even though they hate him."

"Exactly." Lieutenant Fields nodded. "Not a nice man, Mr. Mayfair. But I don't think that vault will open until he gives us the combination."

"A six-letter word will open it, and only Mayfair knows the right word," Porterfield Adams said, puffing pipe smoke. "We could try a hundred thousand words and never hit the right one. Yet, obviously, in spite of all Mayfair's cleverness, someone in this house guessed or discovered the word. It's up to us to do the same."

"Stamps!" Andy said suddenly. They looked at him. "I mean," he said, swallowing a corner of toast, "it's a six-letter word and it's what he was interested in. Maybe it's the code word."

His father shook his head. "Good try, son," he said, "but we thought of that. Also of Africa, where he made his money, Helena, his former wife's name, Castle and Cragie, and lots of others. No go."

"We'll just have to forget the vault," Lieutenant Fields said. "Anyway, if we can arrest the one who shot him, we'll have the thief, too. Apparently your arrival here last night, Porter, alarmed the thief and made him desperate, so he thought he had to kill Mayfair to foil the investigation."

"I wonder . . . " The detective's brows creased still more. "Maybe the thief planned all along to kill him last night and went ahead anyway in spite of my being here."

"You mean because it was the night of the party?" Andy asked. "It was probably the only chance Miss Rainier and Reggie had to get out of the house. And the confusion of a big party would have given them, or even Mr. Muyskens, lots of opportunity to slip out and shoot Mr. Mayfair without their absence being noticed."

"Exactly." His father looked pleased at his deductions. "It put several suspects on the scene and lots of confusion to cover their tracks. No, Dick, this crime was planned. It wasn't a spur of the moment thing. Now I have a sketch here—it shows the layout of the grounds and the path of the bullet."

— 5 —

Adams pushed a sheet of paper into the middle of the table and Andy and Lieutenant Fields studied it.

The Lieutenant nodded. "Good job," he said. "Certainly does seem to pin the shooting on Muyskens, Reggie or Miss Rainier, doesn't it?"

"Straight as an arrow—only there's no way to choose among our three 'mice.' However——"

"Dad!" Andy was almost squirming with eagerness. "The ladder. You have it in the sketch. There, leaning against the end of the west wing."

"Yes?" His father looked at him questioningly. "What about it?"

"I have an idea!" Andy almost exploded with the word. "Please, can we try it? It's about the ladder!"

"Porter, I think your son is becoming a detective," Lieutenant Fields remarked. "Let's have him show us his idea about the ladder, whatever it is."

"Of course." The detective drained his coffee and clapped Andy on the shoulder. "Let's go, son."

It took only a minute or so for them to let themselves out on the paved terrace behind the main hall of the house. They walked around the corner of the west wing of the building and found a heavy, wooden extension ladder leaning against a second-floor window sill.

"The ladder has been there a week," Porterfield Adams

remarked. "A mason started to fix the mortar of the window sill and got sick, so he didn't finish. Now what's your idea?"

"We have to take the ladder down," Andy said. "I wasn't sure it was an extension ladder, but it is—a forty-footer."

"Right. Dick, lend a hand. It'll need us all to get it down."

The ladder was heavy. As they swung it out from the house and balanced it upright, it almost fell. But they caught it and lowered it swiftly. Andy, almost breathless with excitement, pulled the rope that extended the two-part ladder to its full length.

"Now," he said, puffing, "we have to lay it across the moat."

"By George!" Dick Fields looked at him with admiration. "Porter, do you realize neither you nor I ever thought of this ladder being used as a bridge? We thought of other things, but not of a bridge. Your son has shown us we aren't as smart as we thought we were!"

"He certainly has," Porterfield Adams agreed. And as the three of them eased the ladder out, until it lay across the thirty-foot moat, with plenty to spare, he asked, "What made you think of it, son?"

"I saw a ladder in a newsreel used as a bridge to rescue a woman from a burning house," Andy said. "I remembered it. Now look."

He ran lightly across the moat and back, leaping from rung to rung of the ladder in rubber-soled shoes with goat-like agility.

"See?" he cried. "The guilty man doesn't have to be just one of the three who were at the party. Anybody in the house could have got across the moat, sneaked up to steal the rifle, shot Mr. Mayfair, come back, dropped the rifle in the moat, put the ladder back—and pretended to be innocent."

"There's a whole bunch of new headaches for you, Dick," Porterfield Adams chuckled. "New suspects, everything."

"Let's put the ladder back," Lieutenant Fields suggested. "Now, Andy," he said, as they struggled to get the ladder back into position, "the danger with making deductions is that you are apt to make a good one, then stop. It's easy to be so pleased with yourself that you don't look for flaws or further possibilities."

They lowered the ladder with a thump against the window sill and the Trooper dusted his hands.

"Your idea is a good one, a very good one. But take it farther. We three just had a bit of trouble getting that ladder down and up, didn't we?"

"Yes, sir." And Andy suddenly felt crestfallen. How could he have overlooked something so obvious? "You mean, even though one man could handle a ladder like this, it would take him a long time, especially at night? Much too long for anybody in this house to try, especially since dad and I saw Robin and Pardo and Mr. Henderson all upstairs just two or three minutes after the shooting?"

"That's it, boy," Lieutenant Fields nodded. Then Andy had another idea. They seemed to be coming to him thick and fast today. Once he started trying to be a detective, it seemed as if he couldn't turn off his mental machinery.

"Suppose they were all in it together?" he said. "All three of them! Then they could have got the ladder down and up fast, and any of them could have done the shooting—they all know how to handle rifles."

"Wow!" Lieutenant Fields exclaimed. "Porter, another idea we overlooked! If this boy were a few years older, I'd march him back and enroll him in State Troopers school. Even if his ideas aren't right, they're interesting!"

"Well?" Andy scowled, a little belligerent now. "Why isn't that a possible idea?"

"It is a possible idea, Andy," his father said. "And a mighty good one. It could have been worked. But don't forget, Mr. Mayfair suspected someone. He probably had good reason for that suspicion. And he tried to tell us who it was. That was the whole point of the *mice* message he couldn't finish."

For a moment that subdued Andy. Then, being much too worked up with the excitement of detection to be subdued long, he posed a final problem for the two men.

"Maybe," he said, "Mr. Mayfair was trying to say, 'I suspect *my staff*,' meaning Pardo and Sparrow and perhaps Mr. Henderson, too. That would come out *mice*."

Lieutenant Fields started coughing suddenly. Porterfield Adams nodded.

"Son," he said, "if you were the attorney for the defense we might not be able to convict anyone. But there's still another reason why your idea, though it's ingenious, wouldn't work. At least not under last night's circumstances. Can you figure out why?"

Andy thought for a moment. He remembered the darkness, the way the lights had appeared and disappeared as the oak trees were bent over by the wind, and he thought he knew what his father meant.

"You mean, dad," he said, "that it was easy for me to run across the ladder just now in daylight, but at night with a wind blowing a man wouldn't be able to run like that? He'd be apt to step between the rungs and break a leg or fall into the water. He would have to get down and crawl across, and that would take much too long—even if all three of them were in on it. They couldn't possibly have arrived at Mr. Mayfair's room so soon after you called."

"That's it." His father seemed very pleased. "You're

catching on to the art of being a detective fast. In half an hour we're all going to meet in Mr. Mayfair's bedroom, and Lieutenant Fields and I will try to make someone confess. I'm going to let you be there to watch."

While we wait for the stagehands to change scenes—oh, I beg your pardon, this is a book, isn't it? Well, as long as I have started talking, let me ask if you can see any way in which Andy's rather clever notions can be refined or improved upon. May I add that at this point you have all the clues needed to solve the matter of who shot Mr. Mayfair. Think about oak trees in a line. Think about a fat man sitting up in bed, illuminated by a bedside lamp, a perfect target. Think about a November night with the wind moaning like a lonesome ghost and howling like an enraged banshee. Think about a burglar-proof vault with an unknown six-letter combination—think about this hard because it is shortly going to become a matter of life or death. Think about ladders and loud-speakers and a man who wanted to own the rarest stamps in the world. Then turn to page 108 to see attempted murder unmasked, tables turned, and a fantastic puzzle propounded, with someone's life hanging on the right answer.

— 6 —

Andy Adams stood pressed against the wall of Mr.
Nigel Mayfair's bedroom.

The room, big as it was, seemed rather crowded. His
father was there, standing by the bullet-riddled window.
Lieutenant Fields stood beside the locked door to the hall.
Pardo, Robin and a fat man in a white chef's costume
stood ranged on the other side of the bed, looking defiant
or frightened. Mr. Henderson leaned against the wall beside
Andy, smoking and looking intent. Miss Rainier, the only
woman, sat regally at ease in a chair near Porterfield
Adams. Reggie, the stepson, lounged in another chair with
his legs thrust out in front of him and his hands jammed
in his pockets.

"Now, folks," Lieutenant Fields said, "this is an official
part of the investigation into the shooting of Mr. Mayfair.
Mr. Adams is giving us the benefit of some of his
ideas, based on the fact he was here before the crime was
committed. Any questions?"

No one had any. Reggie stirred, as if about to say something, then subsided. Porterfield Adams lifted his hand.

"To begin with," he said, "please notice the string
between bed and window. This establishes the line of flight
of the shots fired at Mr. Mayfair, two of which hit him.
Mr. Muyskens, would you like to sight along the string?"

"Gladly." The tall man with the shock of black hair
stepped forward, sighted for a long minute along the string.

"The line of flight," he said, "goes exactly between two oak trees and ends precisely on the terrace of my home, three hundred yards away."

"Do you have any comment to make about that fact?"

"I do." Muyskens half smiled. "I can only say that it is a brilliant piece of work."

"Meaning what?"

"Anything you choose." Muyskens smiled and returned to his place.

"Miss Rainier." Porterfield Adams turned to the woman. "Do you care to comment?"

She smiled slightly.

"I can only repeat what Howard said—it's a brilliant piece of work."

"And you, Reggie?" Porterfield Adams asked, turning to the younger man. "Any comment?"

Reggie did not bother to stand. He merely smiled, one-sidedly.

"You're not going to get any help from me," he said. "The old boy's dying, and he deserves it. He terrorized us all. You can't prove a thing on me or Howard or Auntie— we were all at the party and all had equal opportunity to fire that shot. Anyway"—and now, to Andy's amazement, he actually grinned—"the whole thing is a pack of nonsense if only you were smart enough to know it."

"An interesting viewpoint," Andy's father said. "You all know about Mr. Mayfair's last words, which sounded like 'I suspect mice—' and by which he might have meant *Muys*kens, or *my s*ister-in-law, or *my s*tepson."

He gave each of them a look, and each returned the look with composure. Andy felt his heart beating anxiously. There was no way his father could possibly pick one of the three as guilty. None whatever.

"You all had motives," the detective went on. "You, Mr.

Muyskens, perhaps to protect the woman you are engaged to. You, Miss Rainier, if you had been stealing his stamps, to prevent his revealing your theft and having you jailed. You, Reggie, the same motive."

"Motive?" the young man sneered. "I had a dozen motives, Mr. Detective. And I'm only sorry I never could guess the word that opens his precious vault. I'd have left long ago and taken his pretty stamps with me."

"However," Porterfield Adams said now, looking briefly at Andy, "I believe I can almost conclusively prove that all three of you are—innocent."

He waited until the buzz of excited exclamation died down, then continued.

"As for how I know," he said, "Old Mother West Wind told me."

He winked at Andy, to whom, when Andy was small, he had read the famous Thornton Burgess stories. And suddenly Andy understood. How could he have been so blind to such an obvious fact?

"That's meant for a little joke," the detective added. "Actually, however, last night a strong west wind was blowing. It tossed the trees badly. When I looked out this window after Mr. Mayfair's shooting, I saw the lights of your house, Mr. Muyskens, appearing and disappearing. The wind was blowing the oak trees beyond the moat so that half the time, or more, they hid this window from sight from your terrace. Tell me, would any marksman hope to hit a man-sized target at three hundred yards in a high wind, with an oak tree still full of dead leaves blowing back and forth across his line of sight?"

"Of course not," Muyskens said. "I wondered if you'd ever think of that. First place, he couldn't estimate the effect of the wind. Second, the waving branches and leaves would distract his sight. Third, there was a good chance the bullets would be deflected by the tree. No, nobody could have shot old Mayfair from my terrace last night."

"Well!" There was actually a look of grudging respect on Reggie's face. "You detective fellows aren't as stupid as I thought."

"Wait a minute." Pardo, the chauffeur and bodyguard, strode forward and sighted along the string attached to the window. "If the shot didn't come from there—it couldn't come from any place. Because it certainly couldn't have come from a window in this house. It would have to come out of thin air!"

"In a manner of speaking," the detective agreed. "And when I realized that, I also realized something else. All of you, please stay well back from the bed. What you are about to see is a demonstration, a reënactment of what happened last night."

He threw up the window and made sure they were all well back. Then he adjusted a fat white pillow on the bed and waved his handkerchief out the window. A moment later Andy saw one of the most unexpected sights of his life.

They were all looking out the windows which adjoined the one the bullets had come through. Now they all exclaimed together as they saw, from just around the corner of the west wing of the building, a ladder appear.

It was the same ladder Andy had seen earlier. Now it was moving out into their sight because it was leaning *away* from the building. And a man straddled the top of it, bracing himself. A man in a State Trooper's uniform. A man who carried a rifle.

Andy expected the ladder to crash. But it didn't. Looking closer, he could see a cord running from the top rung back to the end window of the west wing. The ladder leaned about a dozen feet away from the house—and stopped there, held in position by the cord, which must have been tied to something inside the window.

But who had ever heard—who would ever think—of a ladder leaning *away* from a house. Leaning, you could say, against empty air?

Now the State Trooper on top of the ladder braced himself, holding his position with his legs against the rungs. He raised the rifle to his shoulder. He fired. There was a sharp explosion and feathers flew up in a little geyser on the bed in the room. The bullet had hit exactly where Nigel Mayfair, the night before, had been sitting, reading.

No one bothered to watch the State Trooper descend from the ladder, after which someone inside pulled the ladder back against the house. They were all staring at Porterfield Adams.

"So you see," he said, "how a shot could come from nowhere—out of thin air—and *seem* to have come from somewhere. From your terrace," he added, for Mr. Muyskens' benefit. "But since I knew it almost certainly couldn't have come from your terrace, I tried to read the riddle of the bullet from nowhere. And finally it came to me that the top of that ladder, if it swung away from the house, would neatly come across the bullet's line of flight. And from such a short distance, even in a wind, anyone who knew anything at all about a rifle couldn't miss."

"But that means——" Pardo began. And suddenly they were all looking at Mr. Henderson, who stood close beside Andy, leaning against a door.

"Yes, Mr. Henderson." Porterfield Adams' tone was grim. "That hall window the ladder leans against is just outside your room. In your room is a long electrical extension cord—and those cords are very strong—which shows signs of having been tied around something hot—such as the hot radiator just inside the window. By means of its support you were able to push yourself, on the ladder, away from the window, and remain there, perched, as it were, in mid-air, to shoot Mr. Mayfair.

"No one else could have done the deed in the three minutes that elapsed between the time of the shooting and your appearance. But all you had to do was toss the rifle down into the moat, pull the ladder back against the window, clamber in, and run down the hall to join us. Besides, if anyone else had done it, you would surely have heard the shots and so informed us."

"But he's not a mouse!" It was Andy who spoke. "Dad, he's not a mouse!" Then, blushing crimson, he clamped his mouth shut.

"You mean, son," the detective said, "that his name doesn't begin with s. But Mr. Mayfair is British. And the British call their lawyers 'solicitors.' You heard him call Henderson a solicitor. That's where your 'mice' came from. Mr. Mayfair was trying to say, 'I suspect *my* *s*olicitor'."

Andy gulped. It was true—the wind, the oak tree still full of dead leaves, and the word solicitor—even the ladder, when they held it straight up ten feet from the west wing. He had seen or heard every single clue and failed miserably to deduce the meaning of them. He would never be a detective!

He was startled when Henderson put a strong arm around him. At the same time he felt something hard poking him in the back.

"Alas," Mr. Henderson said. "To be betrayed by a gust of wind. And I thought it was really a very clever plot, too. Or I wouldn't have urged Mayfair to send for you, Adams. But I thought you'd be a little, stoop-shouldered fellow half blind from studying dusty papers, and by actually suggesting you, I persuaded Mayfair he was wrong in suspecting me. That gave me the time I needed to fix up my plan to kill him. Well, under the circumstances, I think it is time for me to say good-by now."

And to Andy's amazement, the door behind them opened. Before any of the others could move, the lawyer dragged him back through it and slammed it shut, and they were in an elevator dropping rapidly downward!

— 7 —

"Mayfair's private elevator," Henderson said. "Don't struggle, boy. I have a gun and I'll use it. Keep calm and you won't be hurt."

The elevator stopped smoothly. The door opened. Henderson shoved Andy out and, still holding him tightly, pulled him across the room so he could lock the heavy door leading into the room.

"The only entrance to the room, and solid oak. It gives us a good five minutes." He grabbed Andy's wrist and twisted it up behind his back. "Over here against the wall, boy, and stand quiet if you don't want a broken arm."

Andy obeyed. Facing away from the wall, he could guess that the man was turning the combination dial of the big vault. He was right, for a moment later it swung open and the lawyer, after clicking on the light inside, marched him in. He sat Andy down in the soft chair that stood behind a desk, and shoved the desk tight against him, pinning him in place.

"Now, my boy," Henderson said, "if you move I have plenty of time to shoot you. If you don't move you have a sporting chance."

He showed Andy the automatic he held, then dropped it into his pocket. Keeping an eye on Andy, he reached for several of the leather-bound loose-leaf stamp albums on the low shelf. Andy did not move. He knew that long before he could get out from behind the desk, the lawyer would have the gun out. Breathing fast, he watched.

"It was a mistake, stealing those first few stamps," the lawyer commented. "But I needed expense money. Now I'll do the job as I planned it all along."

The tall man, humming a little tune, went swiftly through the loose-leaf albums, ripping out plastic strips in which rare and valuable stamps were carefully preserved, and putting them in an envelope. This he put in his pocket and turned. The whole thing hadn't taken a minute.

"There," he said. "Their catalogue value is at least three hundred thousand dollars. I can get a hundred thousand for them in Europe. Well, I must be going. Sorry, but I'm going to have to leave you alone here. Oh, one last job."

He took a small steel box from a shelf.

"This holds Mayfair's evidence against me and the rest," he said. "Everybody will be happy to know I shall burn it."

"You can't get away," Andy said, trying to keep his voice steady. "Listen! They're chopping at the door now."

"So they are. Well, it's worth a try. You see, Andy, I'm going to lock you in here. There's about air enough for five or six hours and no one can possibly unravel the combination in that time. If they agree to give me four hours' head start, I'll telephone your father the combination. Otherwise . . . well, when they get you out, you'll have lost interest in things."

He moved to the vault door and paused, even though outside the vault Andy could hear the sound of an ax being used on the oak door into the room.

"I like you, boy," he said. "I admire your father even though he unmasked me. I was amused by his mention of Old Mother West Wind. So as a sporting gesture I'm going to give you a clue how to figure out the code word to open this vault. Not how I figured it out—for me that was a flash of inspiration—but a clue you can puzzle out while you're waiting. Now listen carefully. I assume you studied some poetry in school. There is a poem called *The Vision of Sir Launfal* written by the poet James Russell Lowell. In it he has one very famous line every school child should know about what makes a June day so perfect.

"Now, I hope you can remember that line, because I'm going to give you a puzzle. Imagine that in the very middle of that June day you are having a picnic, and the menu consists of sausage patties, toasted marshmallows, artichoke heart, mustard pickles and prune whip. If you can solve the puzzle, you'll have a clue to the word which opens this vault. You'll still have to use the clue to figure out the word, so you'll have your work cut out for you. Try thinking about it both forward and backward. And inside out and upside down, if necessary. If that seems bewildering, I can't make it easy, you know, because I do want to get a long way off and hide. If old Mayfair lives, he'll stop at nothing to have revenge on me."

With that he slammed shut the heavy vault door and Andy heard the combination lock turn.

He was alone, in an airtight vault where—if his father couldn't get him out—he would suffocate in a few hours.

Andy shoved the desk away and sprang at the inside of the vault door. He grabbed the handle and twisted it with all his might, in rising panic. His heart was pounding and he seemed unable to get his breath. He couldn't breathe. He was suffocating already!

Then he got hold of himself. He forced himself to be calm. There was air in the vault for several hours, especially if he remained quiet. In that time his father would somehow get the vault open. He was sure of it.

He refused to admit to himself that he wasn't really sure

of it at all, but walked over to the desk and sat down. On the desk were the stamp albums Mr. Henderson had looted of their rarities. He scarcely saw them. He was trying to remember exactly what Mr. Henderson had said, and figure out what he had meant by the puzzle he had left as clue to the word that opened the vault.

A line of poetry about a day in June . . . Something tugged at his memory. He had a vision of himself, memorizing a poem in English class. Not a poem—just a few lines. Something about June . . . Then he had it.

And what is so rare as a day in June?

That was all he could remember. It seemed to mean absolutely nothing. Still, puzzles did seem meaningless until you figured them out. And the solution of this one might save his life.

So he wrote down the line of the poem and then under it the crazy menu Mr. Henderson had specified for the picnic.

And what is so rare as a day in June?

MENU

sausage patties
toasted marshmallows
artichoke heart
mustard pickles
prune whip

He stared at it. It meant nothing as far as he could see. None of the words even had six letters! And it wasn't June and this wasn't a picnic. This was Thanksgiving Day, and he and his father should have been at home, roasting the turkey they were going to cook themselves, since his mother was away. Suddenly tears filled his eyes. He couldn't stop them. He didn't try. Until, unexpectedly, his father's voice spoke.

"Andy! Andy, can you hear me?"

He looked wildly around. But the vault had not opened. The voice was coming from a small round grillwork over the desk. A loud-speaker, such as Mr. Mayfair had all over the house for calling his staff.

"Andy, if you hear me, press the red button under the loud-speaker and answer. Then let go to hear me."

Eagerly Andy pushed the red button.

"Yes, Dad, I hear you."

"Thank heaven for that! Listen, son—we've made a bargain with Henderson. He's to get four hours' head start, then he's to phone me the combination. Do you understand? You'll be all right if you can just keep calm for four hours. The air will last that long, anyway."

"I'll be all right, Dad." Andy said it as firmly as he could.

"We'll be trying to find the combination meanwhile."

"Dad!" Andy interrupted. He told about the clue Henderson had given him, the line of poetry and the picnic with the weird menu. There was a long silence; then his father answered, sounding doubtful.

"That doesn't mean anything I can see," he said. "But we'll get a code expert from the State Police here to work on that angle.

"Meanwhile, stay calm and quiet. We'll be at work and I'll speak to you every few minutes. We can't try to burn open the vault door—you know the reason, don't you?"

"Yes, Dad. I heard Mr. Mayfair say that would flood everything with poison gas."

"Right, son. Maybe you can kill time by looking at the stamp collection. Just don't get impatient."

That was easy to say, but hard to do. Andy looked at

the solid steel walls of the vault all around him, and in his imagination they began to move slowly together as if to crush him. The air seemed to be choking him. His heart pounded, he felt sweat on his forehead. Suddenly he jumped up in a panic and jammed at the red button.

"Dad! Dad!"

"Yes, son?"

He'd been about to ask, *Suppose Mr. Henderson doesn't phone the combination?* But he knew the answer to that. No need to let his father know he was feeling panicky.

"I just wanted to hear your voice."

"Right, Andy. Miss Rainier and Reggie are trying to help us think of words that Mayfair might have used for the combination."

"That's good."

Privately, Andy was sure they would never find it. The fat man had kept the secret word in his head and no place else. Yet, if Mr. Henderson had been able to guess it— well, that proved it could be done. But how could a poem help?

And what is so rare as a day in June . . . sausage patties, toasted marshmallows, artichoke heart, mustard pickles, prune whip . . .

The words seemed to sing in Andy's tired brain, mocking him. They meant nothing, nothing. Why, none of them was even six letters long!

To be doing something, he picked up the nearest red-leather bound loose-leaf stamp album Henderson had thrown down. Outside, in gold, was stamped in large, proud letters:

> *Rarities and Errors*
> *Collection of*
> *Mr. Nigel Mayfair*

Andy opened it. The first page he came to was headed:

British Guiana
One Cent Magenta
Issue of 1856

Below that was a space for the stamp in a plastic envelope, and at the bottom was neatly printed a complete history of the world's rarest stamp, beginning with its finding by a boy named Vaughan, who had sold it for a dollar and a half. Now, as the only existing specimen of the stamp, it was worth at least $50,000.

But obviously Mr. Mayfair had never owned it. The stamp belonged to someone else, and that someone else wouldn't part with it. Just the same, the page indicated that Mr. Mayfair had been determined to own the British Guiana one cent magenta—someday, somehow.

Andy turned to the next pages. They were almost all empty. There were pages which had held the Cape of Good Hope triangular errors, the five important rarities from the island of Mauritius, the rare and coveted U.S. Postmaster Provisionals, the blocks-of-four of the tremendously valuable United States airmail invert error of 1918, a complete collection of the very rare Postmaster Provisional issues of the Confederate States in 1861, and scores more. Mr. Henderson had taken them all.

Wishing he could have seen these rare stamps that were beyond the reach of any but the wealthiest collectors, Andy picked a book from the shelf and made himself look through it. It did help to make him forget that the minutes were ticking away, and with every one that passed there was less air left in the vault for him to breathe.

The book he had selected held a complete collection of United States commemorative stamps in blocks of four.

Ordinarily Andy would have been interested, but now he couldn't study them long. He pushed the book aside, remembering the rage with which Mr. Mayfair had shouted against the postmaster general for reprinting the new Dag Hammarskjöld four-cent error so that it wasn't a rarity any more.

As he pushed the book away, his gaze fell on the sheet where he had written down the line of poetry and the fantastic menu. And—perhaps because he had just been thinking about rare stamps—he suddenly noticed that exactly in the middle of the line was the word *rare*. And Mr. Henderson had said, "In the very middle of that June day." Suddenly the first letter in each line of the menu seemed to leap out at him to spell a word:

And what is so **RARE** as a day in June?

MENU

Sausage patties
Toasted marshmallows
Artichoke heart
Mustard pickles
Prune whip

And at that instant he was sure he knew the word, the one word, that Mr. Mayfair could never have forgotten, must always have been thinking of, and had undoubtedly used as the combination to lock his vault!

Andy punched the red button so hard he hurt his thumb.

"Dad! Dad!" Excitedly he told his father his deduction.

"Good boy! We'll try it. Now don't be disappointed if it doesn't work."

Andy waited, holding his breath. He had to be right. He just had to! But the vault wasn't opening. By now it should have opened. He was wrong! He jabbed at the red button.

"Dad!" he cried. "What's the matter?"

"Sorry, son." His father's voice was carefully controlled. "Your word doesn't seem to work."

Andy held back an impulse to sob. Now suddenly he couldn't get his breath. The air was all gone. He was suffocating!

For an instant Andy almost flung himself at the huge metal door and pounded on it with his fists, as if he could open it that way. The only thing that stopped him was his father's voice—not his actual voice now, but the memory of a time when his father had said, "Always remember, son, the tighter the spot you're in, the more important it is to keep calm and not panic."

Breathing hard, he clenched his fists and tried to think. Mr. Henderson had said something else. What was it? Something about how to think about the puzzle he had given Andy for a clue. What had he said? . . . *Think about it forward, and backward, and inside out and upside down, if necessary.*

"Yes!" Andy shouted out loud. "Backward!"

And he punched the red button again.

"Dad!" he called. "Dad!"

"Yes, son?"

"Dad, try the word I gave you again, but this time spell it backwards!"

"Backwards? But . . . well, all right, we'll try it."

Andy could feel his heart beating like a clock, counting off the seconds while he waited. The clock seemed to be getting louder and louder and faster and faster until——

Slowly the vault door swung open and Andy, like a shot, was out and into his father's firm grip.

"Dad!" he said. "Dad! I was scared I was wrong!"

"So was I," his father said. Then, over his shoulder, "Dick, you can start the chase after Henderson now. He's only had half an hour's head start."

"My men are already phoning to have the roadblocks set up," came the lieutenant's voice. "Why don't you and Andy go in the library where you can talk?"

In the big library, Andy's father put an arm around his shoulders.

"Son," he said, "you did what a real detective does. You read Mayfair's character, and in that way answered a riddle none of the rest of us could. Now—would you care to tell me how you did it? How you finally hit on the word that opened the vault?"

Andy managed a grin.

"Well, Dad——" and he began to feel pleased with himself again as he told how he had found the clue words, *rare stamp,* in the puzzle Mr. Henderson had propounded for him.

"And Mr. Mayfair wanted to be first in everything," Andy concluded. "He wanted to own things no one else did. Like the only genuine castle in America, and the only private moat."

"That's right."

"But there's one stamp so rare there's only one copy of it in the world—a British Guiana stamp. Mr. Mayfair didn't own it. So with Mr. Henderson's clue, I could just imagine Mr. Mayfair brooding all the time about that rare stamp he didn't own and couldn't buy. It would be on his mind constantly. And it was a six-letter word—G-u-i-a-n-a. I decided that it just had to be the word that opened the vault."

"And it was. Even though it had to be spelled backwards."

"Because Mr. Mayfair had a very twisty kind of mind,

Dad. Spelling a word backwards is just the sort of thing he would do. Mr. Henderson gave me a clue to see that, too."

"All the same, Andrew"—Porterfield Adams only used his son's full name when he was especially proud of him—"you did a fine job of making use of the help Henderson gave you. And one of these days I'd kind of like to be able to change the name of my firm to Adams and Son. How would you feel about it?"

"I'd like it," Andy said.

ALFRED HITCHCOCK SPEAKING: *On the above happy note I feel we should close. I don't think we need dwell on the clues which dotted our progress—they have been covered. Perhaps you would like to know about the fate of Mr. Bert Henderson, who escaped so deftly after being, so it seemed, trapped. I am happy to report that a telegram did arrive later giving the code word to open the vault—proving him a man of his word, even though a criminal. But the police did not catch him right away. He went into hiding in the nearest village, where he had already established an identity as a bearded mystery writer who worked nights. He was not caught until January, 1963.*

At that time, you will remember, the postal rates of the U.S. were increased. Going to the local post office, Mr. Henderson gave in to his collector's instinct and bought complete sheets of the new stamps. The postmaster mentioned this to Lieutenant Fields, and soon Henderson was under lock and key. Then the whole story came out.

A lawyer and stamp collector, Mr. Henderson made a slip which brought him into Mr. Mayfair's power. Mr. Mayfair was forcing him to plan to steal the one cent magenta stamp of British Guiana. Instead, he stole Mr. Mayfair's stamps. He richly merited a stern punishment as a warning to others who filch from their friends' stamp collections.

However, when Mr. Mayfair recovered and it became known that some of his own stamps had been stolen from other collectors, he dropped theft charges against Henderson. Of course, the gentleman still has to stand trial for shooting Mr. Mayfair. However, his lawyer has come up with an ingenious defense, so I cannot tell you his final fate at this time.

The Mystery of the Man Who Evaporated

ALFRED HITCHCOCK SPEAKING: *I have a high regard for mystery writers. After all, it is with their help that I have been able to pro- duce my suspenseful motion pictures. I am not, however, altogether at ease around mystery writers. They have active and somewhat sinister imaginations, and I have never met one who did not look at me as if casting me for the role of the stout corpse in his next book. Fortunately, they usually limit their criminal activities to the printed page. As you are about to see, strange things can happen when a mystery writer gets involved in his own plot. . . . Oh yes, there are clues. But can you find them in time to solve——*

The Mystery of the Man Who Evaporated

PRACTICALLY AS LONG AS he had been able to read, Jeff Landrum had enjoyed mystery stories—all kinds. He had thought there wasn't any kind he didn't like. But there was. He realized it now. There was one kind that he didn't care for a bit—the kind of mystery story in which he was one of the characters! Or to be exact—one of the victims.

Jeff chewed desperately at the harsh hemp rope which tied the wrists of his friend together. He was scared but refused to admit it. He had been gnawing at the knot for a good ten minutes, trying to loosen it, and he could feel it just beginning to give.

"Hurry, Jeff!" It was just a whisper, kept low so the man outside the door wouldn't hear. "We haven't got much time."

Jeff didn't stop to answer. He was somewhat plump for his height, but his chubbiness of build did not mean softness. With the determination of a terrier he chewed at the rope, though his lips and tongue felt raw from contact with the rough hemp fibres.

But now the rope was damp from contact with his tongue, and not so hard and slippery. Furiously he sank his front teeth into it. And he felt the end of the knot giving.

"Good boy!" The whisper encouraged him. "Keep it up!"

Jeff gave a jerk of his head and felt the knot loosen some. But before he had a chance to do any more, he heard their captor enter the room. The man came directly to where he and his friend lay on the floor beside the bookshelves, and bent over them. And with sick anticipation, Jeff knew that this fantastic mystery story in which he had got himself involved was about to come to the end. . . .

It had started in the most natural place in the world for a mystery story to begin—at a meeting of The Mystery Writers of America, Inc.

The group known as The Mystery Writers of America, referred to by its members simply as MWA, was an association of most of the mystery writers in the United States. For years Jeff had been reading mysteries without wondering very much about the people who wrote them. When he thought about them at all, he thought of them as being strange individuals who probably lived in lonely old mansions, peering at their typewriters through thick glasses and occasionally getting up to pace to their bookshelves to consult some ancient volume on rare poisons.

It came as a bit of a shock to him to learn that his English teacher, Mr. Howard Matthews, wrote mystery short stories. Mr. Matthews was sandy-haired, with twinkling brown eyes and no need whatever for glasses. He had been a high-jump champion in college, had a very nice wife and three shrieking, roly-poly daughters, and liked to tell funny stories in class.

As soon as Jeff found out that some of the most hair-raising short stories he had read, by an obviously sinister individual named "Daniel Doom," were really the work of Mr. Matthews, he decided he could write one, too.

He promptly set to work and found it was much harder than he had thought. But he kept at it and in a month had finished something that read quite a bit like a story, even though he realized it fell far short of the real thing. He submitted it in English class, and the final result was that Mr. Matthews invited Jeff to drive with him to New York City to attend a meeting of the MWA. Jeff went, keyed up with anticipation.

He was somewhat surprised to find that a group of mystery writers looked just about like any other group of men and women. Some were short, some were tall, some were plump and a couple of the men had beards. They all seemed pleasant and friendly, though anyone overhearing some of the conversations, in which they discussed novel ways of committing murder and disposing of victims, might have been excused for calling the police.

On the other hand, Jeff was tremendously interested in seeing writers who had previously been just names to him suddenly become real people. Erle Stanley Gardner, the creator of the world-famous "Perry Mason," turned out to be a stocky, energetic lawyer who told Jeff how, as a young man, he used his wits to establish the innocence of a

Chinese client. In that way he had won the respect of the whole Chinese community and gained much experience that he later used in his books.

The equally famous Ellery Queen turned out to be two men who worked as a team. Jeff couldn't remember their real names, so he settled for thinking of one as Mr. Ellery and the other as Mr. Queen.

However, the Great Merlini, a tall, thin man whose real name turned out to be something else and who wrote books on magic, actually proved to be a magician himself. When Jeff shook his hand, he was momentarily startled to find himself grasping an unattached hand. The Great Merlini gravely told him he had a very strong grip and asked for his hand back. Then he pulled out a handkerchief that changed into an egg which, when cracked open, produced endless yards of colored ribbon.

The exhibition was ended by an announcement that in the next room an expert from the New York Police Department was starting a talk on identification of blood specimens. This sounded rather interesting, but Mr. Matthews took Jeff's arm and steered him toward the stairs that led down to the excellent French restaurant below, where they had eaten dinner.

"I write suspense-adventure stories, Jeff," Mr. Matthews said, "so I don't need to know anything as technical as blood identification. And I think you'll be more interested in meeting Harley Newcomb. He's downstairs having coffee."

"Harley Newcomb?" Jeff had heard his father mention the name often. His father was a great fan of Newcomb's books. "He's the one who writes mysteries that take place inside locked rooms, isn't he?"

"Locked rooms, sealed rooms, or other places where it doesn't seem possible the crime could have been committed.

He's really a brilliant writer, and the only thing he enjoys is writing. It's hard even to get him to come to these meetings and see his friends. Look at him, there at that table— even now he's writing."

Across the room Jeff saw a small man with rather long, snow-white hair, sitting at a table against the wall, busily scribbling in a large notebook.

"Why, that's the Mr. Newcomb who lives in the cottage on Pete Higgins' farm!" Jeff exclaimed.

"Right. He's practically a neighbor of ours in Laketown. But he keeps to himself because he doesn't want people to know he's the famous Harley Newcomb. He's afraid they'll interrupt his work."

As they approached, Harley Newcomb looked up at them through old-fashioned gold-rimmed spectacles.

"Oh, hello, Howard," he said. "Didn't I see you upstairs?"

"Yes, Harley." Mr. Matthews introduced Jeff. "Still at it?" He indicated the notebook.

"Oh, yes, yes," the mystery writer exclaimed. "Sit down, both of you. It's time for me to stop. Bad habit, writing every place I go."

He tapped the notebook and leaned toward them.

"My fiftieth book!" he said proudly. "What's more, it's going to be one of the most mysterious and puzzling I've ever written."

"Is that so?" Mr. Matthews asked. "Considering the bafflers you've written, Harley, that's saying a lot."

"Here's the situation." The little man leaned toward them, his eyes bright behind his glasses. "The hero, a man, is alone in his country cottage. It has solid stone walls and a concrete floor. There's no fireplace.

"The man telephones a friend and tells him he is experimenting with an old spell he has found in a rare book about magic. The spell is supposed to make someone disappear. Suddenly he shouts, 'Help! Help! I'm starting to shrink!' and the connection is broken."

He chuckled and looked at Jeff. "Then what do you suppose happens?" he asked.

"I don't know, sir," Jeff said. "It sounds terrific, though. Unless it's just a joke."

"A joke!" Harley Newcomb's tone was reproachful. "My stories are never jokes. What happens is that the friend takes the police to the cottage. They find the door locked from the inside. Over all the windows are nailed heavy boards—from the *inside*. When they chop down the door, they find that it, too, has heavy boards nailed over it—all on the inside. The entire cottage has been sealed tight from *inside,* so that not even a mouse could get out. There aren't any trap doors or secret entrances. Nothing like that. Yet— the man has vanished. Completely disappeared. Evaporated into thin air from a room no one could get out of!"

"Gosh," Jeff said, a little awed. "Where do you get your ideas, Mr. Newcomb?"

"Any place and every place," the writer told him, slipping the notebook into his pocket. "This one, as it happens, came out of a conversation with someone I know. That was —let's see, today is the twenty-first. That was on the first of this month, so I've been working on my book only twenty-one days. But I'll have it finished before the end of the month."

He jumped up.

"I've got to get back home," he said. "Just had a new idea, and I'll probably write all night. Come see me next month, Matthews, and bring your young friend."

And the little, white-haired mystery writer hurried away.

"Guess we should start, too, Jeff," the teacher remarked. "It's a two-hour drive."

As they drove back toward Laketown, Jeff mulled over the evening. It had really been tremendously interesting.

"Mr. Matthews," he asked, "do you think I really might be able to write a story that could be published?"

"Sure, Jeff," his teacher answered. "If you want to badly enough. Of course, you have to figure on spending several years or more in learning how. But some writers have gotten started quite young. Robert Bloch, the man you met who wrote *Psycho,* started selling stories when he was seventeen. And you know the book *Frankenstein* of course."

"Yes. It's a terrific story. I saw the movie of it on television."

"Well, it's hard to believe, but it was written by a young woman of nineteen. So you see it can be done."

Jeff tried to decide, during the rest of the drive home, whether he really wanted to write stories, or whether he actually just liked to read them. It was a good thing for his peace of mind that he had no way of knowing that he was soon going to live one—a story more baffling and fantastic than any he had ever read.

The week after his visit to the MWA meeting, Jeff didn't have much time for reading. In addition to his paper route and his homework, he was busy helping the Laketown Athletic Association gather donations for its annual rummage sale. The Athletic Association maintained a Little League baseball field and a summer camp out of the proceeds of the rummage sale, which was so big that it had to be held in a barn and was, therefore, called a Barn Sale.

Several thousand people always came to the Barn Sale, to buy everything from a used refrigerator to a pair of outgrown baby shoes. The job of reminding people to get donations ready, and then getting someone around to pick them up, had to be started weeks ahead of time.

Jeff had reminded every family on his paper route about

the Barn Sale, and had promises of donations of clothes, books, old tools, radios, slightly broken furniture, two refrigerators and even three bales of hay. The heavy items would have to be picked up by men with trucks, but Mr. Matthews offered to drive Jeff in his car and help pick up the other donations on Saturday.

They filled the back of the car and the trunk space with cardboard cartons containing clothing, shoes of all sizes, ages and kinds, tools and books, and then started for Pete Higgins' farm. Pete had the only big, empty barn anywhere near town, so the Barn Sale was always held there.

As they turned into the long lane that led across the farm to the barn, Jeff remembered that the writer he had met, Harley Newcomb, lived in a cottage Pete had built. He wondered out loud if the mystery writer had finished the book he had told them about.

"Probably," Mr. Matthews said. "He told us he'd be finished by the end of the month and this is the thirtieth. He invited us to drop in. Maybe we can stop after we unload the car, and if he's finished he'll tell us some fascinating stories. He used to know Arthur Conan Doyle, who wrote the Sherlock Holmes stories."

They rounded a clump of trees and pulled to a stop in the big, dusty back yard of the rickety, unpainted old farmhouse in which Pete Higgins and his wife lived. A couple of goats tied to trees baaahed at them, and the farmer himself, a heavy-set man of middle age, wearing tattered overalls and badly needing a haircut, looked up and nodded.

Pete Higgins was sawing on a four-by-four timber with which, apparently, he was going to mend the sagging roof of a small lean-to that sheltered his ancient truck. At the moment the corner of the roof was propped up by a stick which wasn't long enough, so it had to be supported in turn by the truck tire jack, which itself was set on some bricks for extra height. The whole thing explained, if you thought about it, why Pete's big barn was always empty and available for the Barn Sale.

Pete just didn't like to work very hard, so he had long ago given up serious farming. Consequently he didn't have anything to keep in the barn.

"Howdy," Pete said, slowly straightening up. "Nice mornin'."

"It certainly is," Mr. Matthews agreed. "Okay for me and Jeff to lug this stuff into the barn?"

"Help yourself," Pete said. "I'd give you a hand, but I got an important job to do here."

Mr. Matthews winked at Jeff.

"We can see that, Pete."

He and Jeff began to carry the cartons into the big barn, which still smelled agreeably of dust and hay. Other collectors had been ahead of them, and already there was a small mountain of rummage waiting to be sorted and put in place for the sale.

"Looks like Pete ought to fall heir to a nice bonus this year." Mr. Matthews chuckled. Instead of paying Pete for the use of the barn, the Athletic Association gave him everything left over when the sale ended. There was always a quantity of clothing left, usually some tools, an old radio or so, maybe a washing machine that could be fixed, old beds, furniture in need of mending, and other discards.

"I wonder what Pete does with all the stuff that's left over," Jeff said as they went for another load. "Do you suppose he sells it?"

"Oh, sure," Mr. Matthews told him. "Pete would much rather sit around fixing an old machine to sell than work his farm. And his wife repairs the old clothes and they sell those, too. Sometimes they get a real windfall—fine quality clothing thirty or even fifty years old, which nobody would dream of buying. Pete keeps that locked up in the loft. Every summer theater in this part of the country knows that when they need costumes for a play, they have a good chance of being able to find them here. Pete charges them good prices, too. What with one thing and another, he makes out. You might not think it to look at him, but he can smell a dollar from a mile away, as his neighbors put it."

They finished carrying the donations into the barn and got back in the car. Pete lifted one hand in a half-hearted good-by.

"Sure sorry I couldn't help," he said. "But chores keep me right busy."

"We'll be back," Mr. Matthews called, and they drove out to the main road. "Now," he told Jeff, "we'll just swing around Pete's wood lot and stop at the cottage to see Harley Newcomb."

By road, the cottage was a quarter of a mile away. It sat by itself well back from the highway, surrounded by trees, in a setting of wooded isolation that helped guarantee the mystery writer from being interrupted.

"Mr. Matthews," Jeff said, as they turned into the driveway, "look! His mailbox is practically full."

"Hmm. So it is." As they got out of the car, the teacher looked back at the large rural mailbox, so full of newspapers and magazines it couldn't even close.

"He hasn't taken in the milk either," Jeff remarked, and Mr. Matthews, staring at the tin receptacle for milk bottles, which now held three bottles of milk, frowned.

"He must be away," he said. "But we'll knock anyway."

He led the way along a gravel path to the front door of the small cottage, which was solidly built of field stones. There was a large knocker on the front door and Mr. Matthews banged it loudly.

There was no answer. He knocked again.

"Take a look in the window, Jeff," he said.

Jeff moved to the nearest window and tried to peer in. His shout of surprise brought the teacher to his side.

Someone had nailed heavy boards over the window from the inside. They were barely an inch apart. Peering through into the dimly lighted interior, Jeff and Mr. Matthews could see no sign of the occupant.

Swiftly they circled the little house, which was only one story high. Every window was boarded up from the inside, and both the front and back doors were tightly locked.

"Jeff," Mr. Matthews said sharply, "run get Pete Higgins! Tell him to bring his extra key to the cottage, and also an ax. We may have to chop our way in. There's something very wrong here."

Jeff was on his way before Mr. Matthews finished speaking. He raced past the garage, a rickety wooden structure which Pete had apparently started to build but never finished. Mr. Newcomb's car stood in it, so obviously Mr. Newcomb hadn't driven away anywhere.

Jeff ran along the path which led through the four-acre wood lot, past a pond, over a brook, and burst into Pete Higgins' back yard, sending a flock of chickens flapping with a great cut-cutt-cutta-cawing.

"Mr. Higgins!" he shouted. "Come quick. Mr. Newcomb is gone!"

Pete Higgins straightened up with surprising speed.

"Gone!" he said. "Without payin' me th' rent? He can't do that!"

"We're afraid something's happened to him," Jeff explained breathlessly. "Bring your key to the cottage, and an ax, too. And hurry!"

Impressed by his tone, the farmer grabbed an ax from the nearby chopping block.

"Got the key on my ring," he said, displaying an enormous bunch of keys of every shape and size. "What'd you say happened to the writer feller?"

"We don't know, but the cottage is all boarded up from inside."

Running together—though the farmer did not run very fast—they got back to the cottage to find Mr. Matthews peering through one of the windows.

"I still can't see any sign of him," the teacher reported. "Pete, try to open the front door."

"You bet!" Pete Higgins said emphatically. "It's in the lease he can't go away 'thout payin' me the rent in advance."

He fumbled through the immense bunch of keys and finally found one which fitted. He tugged at the door but it wouldn't budge.

"Something wrong." He frowned. "Door solid as a rock. And look—there's nails sticking through from inside."

He pointed and Jeff saw them now—the sharp tips of nails hammered into the door.

"He must have boarded up the door, too," he suggested to Mr. Matthews, who was looking very grim.

"Yes. That means you'll have to chop it down, Pete."

"Now wait a minute. Just wait a minute. Doors cost money, mighty good money."

"We've got to get inside! Obviously something has happened to Harley Newcomb. When did you see him last, Pete?"

"See him last?" The farmer scratched his stubbly chin and frowned with the effort of remembering. "Oh, sometime last month, I expect. 'Bout six weeks ago. Phoned me, said a faucet was leakin'. He didn't like to be bothered, so I never went around 'less he phoned."

"Six weeks ago, eh? And we saw him in the city ten days

ago. At a guess, I'd say his mail and milk haven't been taken inside for a week now."

"Let's see, three bottles of milk, he got one quart every two days, that would be six days——" Pete Higgins mumbled. "Just about a week, yes, that seems right, Mr. Matthews."

"Then apparently something happened to him about three days after he came back from the city. He may be inside now, sick or——Anyway, we've got to get in. Break a window if you don't want to break down the door."

"Well, okay, glass is cheaper 'n doors," Pete said.

He moved over to the nearest window and with the back of the ax he shattered the glass. Then he swung the ax against the stout boards which covered the window on the inside. It took a dozen blows to loosen them.

"Nailed on mighty tight," he puffed. "But they're comin'. There. One end's loose. Now we can push 'em back far enough to crawl in. You go first."

"All right," Mr. Matthews said. "Hold the boards back."

With the farmer pushing back the boards he had loosened, Mr. Matthews was able to slide inside. Then he pulled the boards back to leave an opening through which he helped Jeff and Pete Higgins.

Inside, the boarded-up windows made the big living room almost dark. Jeff blinked, trying to see better. Mr. Matthews raised his voice.

"Harley! Oh, Harley!" he called. There was no answer. "Let's turn on the lights," he said.

He clicked the nearest switch. Nothing happened. The room stayed almost dark, except that Jeff's eyes were readjusting now and he could see on the walls a collection of devil masks from the South Seas. They looked like evil demons scowling down at him. Bookshelves filled all one wall, and in the middle of the shelves was a cleared space where three human skulls, one big, one medium-sized and one small, sat side by side and grinned at them.

"I don't like this," Pete Higgins said, lowering his voice uneasily. "I don't like it one little bit."

"Come on," Mr. Matthews said. "He might be in the bedroom."

He started for the bedroom, the only other room in the house except for a tiny kitchen and bath. Pete Higgins followed. Jeff saw a pair of candles on a table, and a cigarette lighter. With a flame from the lighter he got the candles burning and lifted them to look around.

The flickering candles sent strange shadows dancing around the room, making the devil masks on the wall, with crisscrossed native spears under them, seem to leer and wink.

Holding the candles high, Jeff approached a big desk that held a typewriter. On the desk beside the typewriter was a large book, open. Obviously it was very old, and it seemed to be printed in Latin. Jeff couldn't read it—but he could read the sheet of white paper in the typewriter.

There was just one line of typing on it.

Help! Help! I'm starting to shrink . . .

That was all. But just reading it gave Jeff goose flesh all over.

"Mr.—Mr. Matthews," he called.

The teacher and Pete Higgins came back in from the bedroom.

"He's not in there," Mr. Matthews said. "Windows boarded up just as tight as in here."

"I tell you," the farmer was arguing, "whoever boarded up these windows and doors has just got to be still inside. Couldn't a cat get out of this place."

"But Harley Newcomb is gone," Mr. Matthews retorted. "Good boy, Jeff. Those candles help. But you look pale."

"This—this message in the typewriter," Jeff said. "And this book. It's very old and it's in Latin——"

Mr. Matthews read the typewritten line, then he studied the old book.

"It's in Latin, all right," he said, "and must be four hundred years old. I can't read it very well, but this page seems to be a spell for—making a man disappear."

Jeff swallowed hard. That was what he had been afraid of.

"Give me a candle!" Mr. Matthews said. "I'm calling the police."

He carried a candle over to the telephone, picked up the receiver and dialed. He waited a moment, then bent down to look at the telephone wire. It had been cut.

"Somebody cut the telephone wire and removed the light fuse!" he said grimly and stopped. He was staring at something on the floor, something just beyond the chair the mystery writer would have sat in to use his typewriter. Jeff leaned over to look, too. There on the floor was a large, irregular red stain.

"Blood," he gasped.

"No," Mr. Matthews said. "Red ink. Here's a bottle that got knocked over and spilled. The fact the ink has dried means it happened several days ago, probably a week. But look. Here's a footprint. As if Harley jumped up from the chair, stepped into the ink, and started running."

"And here's another footprint." It was Pete Higgins, who had grabbed the other candle from Jeff and was bending close to the floor a few feet away. "And here's another. And another. And two more. Six in all. But look at 'em, Mr Matthews, look at 'em and tell me—tell me I'm not seein' right."

The teacher and Jeff crowded close to study the six crimson footprints, all made by someone stepping into the red ink when it was wet.

And Jeff felt a prickling sensation around the roots of his hair.

The first footprint was that of a normal-sized man. The second print was only of the sole of a shoe, as if the man who made it had been running. But it was smaller than the first footprint. And each of the remaining prints was successively smaller than the one before it, until the last was small enough to have been the footprint of a little child.

"He was runnin'!" Pete Higgins' Adam's apple shot up and down in agitation, and his voice was a hoarse whisper. "He was runnin' toward the bedroom and he kept gettin' smaller as he ran. Then—then it looks like he just plain disappeared. Like he—he evaporated!"

They looked at each other, and Jeff had a hard time keeping his voice steady.

"Mr. Matthews," he said. "Remember the story Mr. Newcomb told us at the meeting? About the man who is locked into a cottage and vanishes while trying out a magic spell? His story—his story has come true!"

Ah—I hope I'm not intruding. But I feel I would not be doing my duty if I did not tell you that several significant clues to the strange problem of the man who evaporated have been given you. However, they are of a subtle nature, and if you cannot imagine how a man could vanish from a cottage tightly sealed on the inside, or how an ancient magical spell could make him shrink into nothingness, cheer up—neither could the police. But then, the police are so seldom called upon to solve such problems these days!

Mr. Matthews went to call the State Police from Pete Higgins' phone, while Pete and Jeff kept watch outside the empty cottage. Neither of them cared to wait inside. Pete muttered several times about the unfairness of Harley Newcomb in disappearing without paying his rent, but he did it half-heartedly. He walked around the cottage several times, staring at it and shaking his head, as if half expecting to see a door he had never noticed before. Jeff walked with him, but no amount of staring changed anything. It still remained a solid stone cottage with a slightly overhanging roof that showed no break or opening of any kind.

Presently Mr. Matthews came back, and immediately after him arrived the first State Police car. As soon as the officers had sized up the situation, they radioed the nearest barracks and before long there were five police cars on the scene, and uniformed men were swarming over the premises.

They took down the boards Pete had loosened, but left all the rest in place for photographing and study. And Jeff had the excitement of watching a full-fledged police investigation for the rest of the day.

They tapped the walls with hammers, tested the boards nailed over the windows, and even crawled up on the roof to make sure all the shingles were tight.

They learned that the boards which covered the doors and windows on the inside had come from a large pile beside the garage Pete had never finished. The nails had come from a keg of rusty nails beside the boards. And the hammer that had been used was an old one that Pete had left handy, just in case he ever got around to finishing the garage. So anyone at all could have made use of the tools and the boards. There were no clues there.

Otherwise, the investigation left everything just where it started. It seemed plain that not even a cat could have got out of the sealed-up cottage. Just the same, Harley Newcomb had disappeared. And much as the police wanted to find some secret exit or trap door in the roof, they couldn't. As Pete Higgins kept saying to them plaintively:

"I tell you fellows, there just ain't any secret trap doors or foolishness like that. I ought to know. I built this here cottage with Joe Caruso, my hired hand, back five, six years ago. Solid stone and mortar for th' walls. Good thick concrete for the floor. Nice tight roof, never leaked. Mr. Newcomb lived here ever since. Never had a mite of trouble with him until now, when he's gone and evaporated and not paid th' rent. People shouldn't fool around with magical spells—stuff like that can be dangerous."

The State Police obviously weren't satisfied, but they couldn't discover any trace of Harley Newcomb. The famous mystery writer was gone. And if he hadn't evaporated, then he had vanished in some way just as mysterious.

The police finally decided that Harley Newcomb had disappeared on purpose—to get publicity, but nobody else believed that, especially Mr. Matthews.

"That's nonsense, Jeff," he said as he drove Jeff home late in the afternoon. "Harley hated publicity. He went out of his way to avoid it."

"Do you think that—that the magical spell really had anything to do with it at all?" Jeff asked.

"No, of course not." But the teacher did not seem as positive as the words sounded. "Frankly, I don't know what to think. It would help a lot if we had the slightest idea how he got out of that cottage. Or—I hate to say this— how his body was taken from it."

"You think somebody——" Jeff began.

"I don't know. I hope not. But I'm afraid it's possible. This much I'm sure of. Somebody else—not Harley Newcomb—is behind the whole thing. Yet as far as I know, he didn't have any enemy in the world."

"Suppose he was trying out his plot idea, the one he told us about, to make sure it would work," Jeff argued. "And maybe he got hurt or something."

"Then we'd have found some trace of him," the teacher said. "Frankly my head is spinning. I'm going to sleep on it. You know the police found no trace of the book he was supposed to be writing. They phoned New York, and his publisher said he didn't mail it in. Do you realize what that means?"

"N-no." Jeff scowled. "I don't think so."

"It means the manuscript he was writing was stolen," Mr. Matthews said. "And who would want to steal an unfinished mystery book?"

"I don't know," Jeff admitted.

"Neither do I. Unless it was because the manuscript would tell us the secret of how Harley Newcomb vanished. Well, here's your house, Jeff. See you in school Monday. By then maybe the police will have learned something."

But by Monday the police knew little more. And Harley Newcomb had still not been found. So the police stuck to their theory that the writer was just trying to get publicity.

The newspapers, though, ignored this theory. Both the New York papers and the local paper carried big stories and pictures that made the whole thing sound like black magic. The headlines were large and exciting. Some of them said:

DID FAMOUS MYSTERY WRITER EVAPORATE INTO THIN AIR?

WRITER LIVES OWN STORY— VANISHES FROM SEALED ROOM

ANCIENT BLACK MAGIC SPELL SHRINKS WRITER TO ZERO!

The old Latin book of magical spells, the skulls on the bookshelf, the native devil masks and spears, all made wonderful pictures. And the way in which the news stories were written certainly did suggest that something strange and diabolical must have taken place inside that cottage.

There were photographs of the footprints, showing how they got progressively smaller, and of the message for help in the typewriter. There were even photographs of Jeff and Mr. Matthews and Pete Higgins. Jeff was kept busy telling the story to all his friends.

The whole community was consumed by curiosity, and so many townspeople, and others from New York, drove out to see the cottage that the police had to direct traffic. They also had to post a guard around the building to keep curiosity seekers from getting in to look for souvenirs. Pete Higgins began patrolling around the cottage with a shotgun.

"If he don't come back to pay the rent," he declared, "everything he left behind belongs to me for security. Nobody's goin' to lift as much as a nail from that there cottage."

After three more days, the newspapers began to lose interest and the police, unable to discover anything, withdrew, declaring it was all a publicity stunt. But still people flocked to see the "mystery cottage," as everyone now called it. Pete Higgins, with his usual shrewdness for making a dollar, called on a cousin to help him put up a big sign that said:

$1   SEE THE MYSTERY COTTAGE $1
See the Message for Help!
See the Crimson Footprints!
$1   THE PUZZLE OF THE CENTURY $1

He built stairs so people could crawl in through the window, but left everything else exactly as it was. With his cousin on guard inside to see that nothing was stolen, he stood outside and collected a dollar admission from scores of curious sightseers.

By the end of the week, his neighbors estimated he had made at least two hundred dollars, and they all shook their heads admiringly at Pete's ingenuity.

Gradually the excitement died down but, busy though he was, Jeff could not stop thinking about Harley Newcomb's uncanny disappearance. After all, Jeff had helped discover the mystery—now he yearned to solve the puzzle of what had really happened. Then it occurred to him he had a clue the police didn't know about—a clue he had forgotten!

That day after school he bicycled to the State Police barracks to tell the clue to the lieutenant in charge. He explained how Harley Newcomb had been talking to him and Mr. Matthews about the book he was working on, and how Newcomb had told them that he got the idea from a casual conversation with someone he knew. He had even mentioned that the conversation took place on the first of the previous month.

"Don't you see?" Jeff asked eagerly. "If you could find who it was Mr. Newcomb got his idea from, you might have the answer to how he could disappear from that sealed-up cottage."

The uniformed officer smiled at him.

"We appreciate your trying to help, son," he said, "but look at it this way. Mr. Newcomb disappeared in exactly the way the man in his book was going to disappear. Right?"

Jeff nodded.

"Well, then, isn't it obvious the whole thing is a plan to draw attention to the book when it comes out?" the officer asked. "Just a publicity stunt, pure and simple."

"But the book is missing," Jeff argued stubbornly. "It wasn't in the cottage and the publisher hasn't received it."

"That's because Mr. Newcomb, wherever he is, has it with him, finishing it up," the officer said. "You'll see, one of these days the book will be published and Mr. Newcomb will reappear and get lots more publicity. I'm sorry, but people are always pulling stunts to get free space in the newspapers."

Jeff left, feeling let down, but not convinced. He stopped by Mr. Matthews' home and found the teacher correcting exams. He told Mr. Matthews his idea.

"That's good thinking, Jeff," the teacher said. "I'd really forgotten that. But since we can pinpoint the conversation to one particular day, and we know that Harley Newcomb hardly ever went anywhere except on the first of the month, when he came into town to shop and buy stamps and things, it's just possible you might be able to find out who gave him the idea—and what the idea was. If we knew the secret of how he got out of that cottage—or was taken out —we'd be a lot closer to solving the mystery. Why don't you ask around? You can do it in a natural way without arousing too much curiosity."

"A lot of people really think Mr. Newcomb did evaporate —shrink to nothing," Jeff said. "Because of those footprints and all."

"I know. But I still don't believe in black magic. Well, good luck, Jeff. Let me know if you learn anything."

Jeff went out and got on his bicycle and rode into town in a thoughtful mood. Would anybody remember a conversation that took place almost six weeks before?

He arranged with a friend to deliver his papers, then he went first to Mr. Martino's grocery, because that was where Harley Newcomb always bought his groceries. Mr. Martino, a fat, jovial man with a large handle-bar mustache, listened intently to Jeff's question.

"Talk?" he asked. "*Si*, we talk, him and me. He say he got to hurry home, got to get started writing. He have a wonderful new idea. That help any, Jeff?"

"What time was this?" Jeff asked eagerly. So Mr. Newcomb already had his idea when he came to the grocery!

"After lunch. Mebbe three, mebbe three-thirty, hard to remember."

"Thanks a lot!" Jeff hurried out. He went next to the post office, where old Mr. Rogers, the thin, bald postmaster, took time to listen to him.

"Hmmm," the postmaster said, tugging at his ear. "Now let's see, when was that writer fellow in last? I 'member he sent a registered letter—s'pose I check the records."

Jeff waited with a fast-beating heart as Mr. Rogers leafed through some records and came back.

"That was it, all right," he said. "First of last month. One-thirty P.M."

"And did you talk about writing stories or anything?" Jeff asked. The postmaster shook his head, his gold-rimmed spectacles slipping down his nose.

"He was in a mighty big hurry," he said. "Wanted to get that registered letter off to some bookstore in New York selling rare old books!"

"Thanks!" Jeff said, and hurried out again. To him it

sounded as if Mr. Newcomb must have been mailing a letter to order that book on magic which had been found on his desk. Which meant he already had his idea and was getting together material he would need to help him write it. Then he must have talked to someone else, still earlier that day. But who?

Jeff tried the library, the drugstore, the telephone company office where Mr. Newcomb had stopped to pay his bill. At each place he learned Mr. Newcomb had been in a hurry. He had told the librarian to be on the watch for his next book, which was going to be specially good. That was at eleven in the morning.

Jeff was stumped. He had seen all the people Mr. Newcomb usually talked to. Mr. Newcomb must have just bumped into someone on the street, someone there was no way of tracing.

Dejectedly, he went home and had his supper. His father and mother noticed he was unusually silent, but they were hurrying to drive over to visit some friends for the evening, and they didn't ask him why. Jeff ate, did some homework, checked his accounts for his paper route, and went to bed early.

He lay there in the darkness, his arms behind his head, his mind buzzing with thoughts. Who could Mr. Newcomb have talked to that day when he got his wonderful idea? Who else in town would he have been apt to see?

And then Jeff sat up suddenly in bed.

"Of course!" he said out loud. "That's who! It has to be."

Without even stopping to think, he hurried into his clothes. His father and mother wouldn't be home for an hour or more. He tore a sheet of paper from a notebook and scrawled on it: *I had to go out but I'll be home soon. Don't worry. Love, Jeff.* He put it on his bed and went out, closing the door, not stopping to think that when they came home they would see his door shut, assume he was asleep, and not look in.

He got his bicycle off the porch, turned on the headlight, and wheeled it down the steps. A moment later he was pedaling as fast as he could pump toward Mr. Matthews' house on the outskirts of town.

Rolling up Mr. Matthews' driveway a few minutes later, he saw that the living room light was still on. He ran up on the porch and through the window could see the teacher, still busy correcting the mid-term themes and examinations. Apparently Mrs. Matthews and the girls were asleep, so Jeff tapped lightly on the glass. Mr. Matthews came over, saw who it was, and let him in.

"Mr. Matthews," Jeff panted, "I think I know who Mr. Newcomb talked to that day and maybe got his idea from!"

"Well, now," Mr. Matthews said thoughtfully. "So you found out something this afternoon?"

"Not yet. But I *figured* out something," Jeff said. "To be positive, I have to ask Pete Higgins a question. I wondered if you thought we could drive over tonight?"

"Tonight. Isn't it rather late?"

"I know it's late, but gosh, if I'm right, it might give us the clue we need!" Jeff said breathlessly. "I won't be able to get to sleep until I know if I'm right or wrong."

"I see." Mr. Matthews chuckled. He got his jacket and slipped it on. "In that case, let's go ask Pete your question. Don't count on his remembering anything that happened more than a month ago, though."

He got out his car and they started toward Pete's farm. The teacher was tempted to ask Jeff what his idea was, but Jeff was obviously so keyed up with excitement and the desire to surprise him, that he refrained. He did ask casually:

"You think maybe someone called on Harley Newcomb that day and perhaps stopped to ask Pete how to find the cottage where he was living?"

"Something like that," Jeff said. He was bursting to tell the idea that had come to him, and at the same time he was eager to surprise Mr. Matthews. He ended up by saying nothing until, as they neared the farm, he saw a light shining ahead and realized they were on the road which passed the mystery writer's cottage on the way to the farm.

"Mr. Matthews!" he exclaimed. "Look—there's somebody in the cottage now!"

"So there is." The teacher turned in the driveway. "It's probably Pete. I understand he's fixing it up to make it a regular exhibit and charge admission all summer. He expects to make a lot of money."

They stopped and got out. Jeff was hardly able to restrain his impatience. Through the window they could see Pete Higgins, still in his tattered overalls, moving around the room.

"Hello, Pete!" Mr. Matthews called. "Can we come in?"

The farmer came to the window and looked out, blinking.

"A dollar each admission," he said. "Men, women, or children . . . Oh it's you and Jeff, Mr. Matthews. I reckon," he finished grudgingly, "you can come in 'thout payin' admission."

"Thanks." The teacher crawled through the window and Jeff followed him. "Doing pretty well here with sightseers, I understand, Pete."

"Not bad," the farmer allowed. "Keeps a man humpin', though, makin' sure nobody steals nothin'."

Jeff looked around curiously. The interior was pretty much as it had been the day they discovered the strange mystery. But Pete had placed protective glass over the crimson footprints and put fancy ropes along the bookcases and beside the prints to keep anybody from getting too close.

And he had moved the three human skulls that had been on the bookshelf. One now stood right beside the typewriter. One sat on top of Mr. Newcomb's big unabridged dictionary. One remained on the shelf. He had also apparently added a couple of extra-ugly devil masks to the ones on the wall.

"Just fixin' things up a bit," Pete said, as they looked around. "Make 'em more interestin', you know. So folks'll feel they got their dollar's worth."

"What'll you do if Mr. Newcomb comes back?" Mr. Matthews asked.

"Oh, he won't come back," the farmer said confidently. "I mean, it stands to reason, if he was comin' back he'd be back by now. I tell you, that magical spell went wrong and he just plain evaporated."

"I hope not," Jeff's teacher said. "But Jeff has a question for you. Go on, Jeff, ask Pete whatever it is you want to know."

For a moment Jeff hesitated. Suddenly he had a strange feeling that he was doing something very foolish, trying to discover the key to the mystery all by himself. But the words were on the tip of his tongue and they came out in a rush.

"Mr. Higgins, you talked to Mr. Newcomb the first of last month, didn't you?" he asked.

And the teacher beside him suddenly snapped his fingers.

"Of course you did, Pete! I know you said you hadn't seen him for several weeks, but you must have talked to him that day. You're his landlord, and I'm sure you wouldn't miss calling on him on the first of the month to collect the rent!"

"And while you were talking to him, you gave him an

idea!" Jeff burst out. "You gave him an idea for a new book. You're the only one who could have because by the time he got into town, he was already planning how he'd write it!"

Pete Higgins' wind-reddened face turned dark and angry. His eyes glared and his lips tightened.

"Yes, by grab, I did!" he rumbled. "Come over here that mornin', I did, to get the rent check. Newcomb, he was pacin' up and down like a cat on hot bricks. Said he had a book to write and couldn't think of a plot. Said he needed a real smart way to get out of a room all locked up. Said he'd give five hundred dollars for a good idea, he did!"

As he spoke, the farmer's face grew more and more flushed, and his eyes glared even more angrily. His big hands opened and closed. Jeff had heard that Pete had a temper, but this was the first time he had ever witnessed it. Pete seemed to be working himself up into a fury.

"And you gave him an idea, eh?" Mr. Matthews spoke quietly, as if trying to calm Pete.

"You bet your boots I did," Pete said. "I gave him a humdinger of an idea. A real humdinger. And he said he'd think about it, that probably it had been used before. So I figured he ought to know, and I left. But then, along toward the end of the month, I dropped in to ask if he'd been thinkin' about it, and he was busy typin'. I saw a couple of the pages and he was using my idea, lock, stock and barrel! I asked him for the five hundred he'd promised and he said the idea wasn't worth it. He offered me fifty."

"Well, what did you do, Pete?" Mr. Matthews asked very quietly, while Jeff watched with rising anxiety as the other man got more and more worked up.

"I told him to give me five hundred or else!" Pete roared. "And he said that was ridiculous. So I showed him how ridiculous it was."

"How?" the teacher asked, trying to distract the farmer.

"I'll show you how!" Pete Higgins bellowed. And before Mr. Matthews could duck, he lashed out with a big fist that caught the sandy-haired teacher on the chin and knocked him backward to the floor.

Jeff knew he had to get help fast, and he darted around Pete. He almost made it to the window. But Pete reached out and caught him by the belt, hurling him to the floor. That was the last thing Jeff knew for several minutes.

I'm rather proud of Jeff for realizing at last that the one person you're apt to see on the first of the month is your landlord. I wonder if any of you, noticing how eager Pete was for money, realized that he'd never let the first go by without collecting the rent? If you did, you're probably way ahead of us now and know the entire secret of the sealed cottage, the man who evaporated, and the crimson footprints. You've had a number of good clues . . . still, you could be wrong. One thing is plain, though—Jeff made a bad mistake in not telling Mr. Matthews what he had in mind. I have an uneasy feeling that Pete Higgins may have some rather drastic plans in mind for Jeff and Mr. Matthews. Why not turn the page and find out? At the same time you can see if your deductions about the disappearance are correct.

CONCLUSION

Jeff opened his eyes groggily. It took him several seconds to realize where he was and what had happened. Then he tried to sit up, and immediately lay back with a muffled, "Ouch!" His head hurt. So did his wrists and ankles. Of course he had bumped his head, but his wrists hurt because they were tied behind him. His ankles were also tied, with a coarse quarter-inch hemp rope. He was lying on the floor on his side, near the bookshelves, and beside him was Mr. Matthews.

"Jeff? Are you all right?" the teacher asked anxiously.

"I guess so," Jeff said. "Did Pete Higgins tie us up?"

"Like a couple of chickens for market." The teacher's tone was grim. "Tied us up and left us here and went off, saying he'd be back."

"What—what do you think he intends to do?" Jeff tried to sound brave, but he didn't feel that way in the least.

"I'd rather not guess. If he were a reasonable man, I could talk to him. But he's not reasonable. You saw what a fury he got into when he told how Newcomb refused to pay him the money he'd promised."

"Yes," Jeff said.

"I'll try to talk to him, but he doesn't act like a man who'll listen now. Jeff, I've been trying to loosen the knot around my wrists. If I turn my back to you, do you think you could untie the knot with your teeth?"

"I'll try, Mr. Matthews," Jeff told him.

The teacher turned on his side, and Jeff wriggled himself down until he could see Mr. Matthews' bound wrists. Pete had tied a tight knot, and Jeff was doubtful if the scheme would work, but he wasted no time. He caught the top strand of the rope between his front teeth and began to tug at it, worrying it like a puppy with a slipper.

All that happened was that his teeth slipped, and the rough rope hurt his lips. Doggedly he tried again. This time he got a better hold on the rope. He was desperately trying to loosen it when they heard heavy footsteps outside.

Pete Higgins was back!

But he did not come inside. He was pushing a wheelbarrow—they could hear the crunch of the wheel on gravel. They heard him stop. Then they heard a metal sound, followed by a wooden thumping noise. Then, after a moment, came a strange new sound—the click-click of a truck tire jack being levered slowly up.

"What do you think he's doing?" Jeff whispered. They were facing the wall and could not see toward the open window.

"I don't know, but keep working on that knot, Jeff. Maybe he'll give us enough time."

Frantically, Jeff worked at the knot with his teeth. Outside, they could hear the slow, steady click-click of the jack. And then a new, strange sound—a creaking of timbers that accompanied each click.

Jeff couldn't guess what it was. He chewed desperately at the rope which tied Mr. Matthews' hands. Five minutes passed, and then ten, and at last he could feel the knot beginning to give slightly.

"Hurry, Jeff!" the teacher whispered. "We haven't much time."

The strange sound of the auto jack and the creaking timbers had ceased now, and he could hear Pete Higgins moving around outside. Jeff's lips and tongue were raw from contact with the rope. But by now it was damp, and not so hard and slippery. Furiously he sank his teeth into the knot and pulled. And he felt the end of the knot give.

"Good boy!" the whisper encouraged him. "Keep it up!"

Jeff gave a last tug and felt the knot loosen. But at that same moment Pete Higgins lowered himself heavily into the cottage through the window and tramped across the room toward them.

Swiftly Mr. Matthews rolled over on his back to hide the fact his hands were partly loose, and Jeff did the same. The farmer bent over them, looking grim.

"All right, you two," he rumbled, "I guess I'm ready to take care of you."

Jeff heard the words, but their meaning didn't sink in because his gaze was fastened to the corner of the cottage where the roof rested on the stone walls. It was a beamed ceiling, with the rafters exposed. And to Jeff's astonishment, the whole roof at that corner had been raised about twelve inches. A distinct gap showed between the roof and the stout stone wall of the cottage.

Mr. Matthews saw it, too, and he spoke swiftly, trying to distract Pete's attention.

"So that's the answer!" he exclaimed. "Pete, that's really very clever. Instead of any secret exits, you just lifted the roof enough so that a man could squeeze through and get out, after boarding up all the windows and doors from inside. Then you lowered the roof again and everything looked normal. We should have figured that, though a roof looks as if it were solidly attached to a house, it really sits on top of the house and isn't always fastened down as tightly as it should be."

For a moment his ruse worked. Pete Higgins chuckled.

"That's right," he said. "My hired hand Joe did all the mason work on this here cottage. He was a good worker. Me, I did the carpenterin', and I ran out of nails when I

got to that end of the roof. It was too much trouble to go to town to get me some more. So that end weren't really fastened. I figgered a truck jack under a four-by-four beam would lever the end up real easy, and I was right. That was the idea I gave Mr. Newcomb that he said wasn't any good."

His face turned black with anger again.

"But I showed him how good it was!" he said. "I did it and fooled the police and everybody, didn't I? Nobody ever came close to stumbling on it."

"You certainly did," Mr. Matthews said. "You really fooled us. But tell me—those footprints that got smaller. How on earth did you manage that?"

"Easiest thing in the world. I got all kinds of shoes, all sizes, left over from old Barn Sales. I got me different size boys' shoes, plus one of Mr. Newcomb's, and just wet 'em in the ink and pressed 'em down for the footprints. Then I typed that message on the typewriter. And those newspapers! How they wrote up them stories about the man who evaporated!"

He guffawed. "Most fun I had all my life, watching everybody come and go, trying to figure it out."

"When you explain it, it all sounds very simple," Mr. Matthews admitted. "But what did you do to Harley Newcomb?"

"Oh, he's still up in my barn loft. I keep it locked because I got all the old costumes up there," Pete told him. "His book's there with him that he stole from my idea. I was waiting to see if anybody would guess it was me who boarded up his cottage from inside and then climbed out through the space under the roof, then let the roof down again. But nobody did. So now I can go ahead with my plans."

His voice had suddenly turned so cold and ominous that

Jeff shivered.

"Now listen, Pete," Mr. Matthews said. "You haven't really hurt Mr. Newcomb or us. Let us go and release him, and it won't be too bad for you."

"Let you go?" Pete Higgins looked astounded. "When you know the whole secret, and would tell and spoil everything? Do I look crazy or something?"

"Now, Pete, you'd better think twice before——"

"I don't have to do any thinkin'!" the other man roared. "At first, I only figgered to hide Mr. Newcomb long enough to show him how good my idea really worked, and teach him not to try to cheat folks. But then people started wantin' to see the mystery cottage, and I saw how I couldn't let Mr. Newcomb go after all. Because I took in four hundred dollars already, in less'n a week, and I ain't lettin' him spoil that."

"Now listen, Pete——" Mr. Matthews began, but the farmer shouted him down.

"No, you listen to me. I ain't lettin' him spoil this nice little gold mine I got, and I ain't lettin' you two spoil it either. No siree! Instead, you're goin' to make it better for me. Why, after they find this cottage all boarded up again, and break in and find you two inside, it'll be the biggest mystery of the whole century. I bet you I take in a hundred dollars a day. Pretty near a thousand dollars a week."

"What do you mean, after they find us?" Mr. Matthews demanded. And Jeff, who had wanted to ask the same question, watched with a dry mouth and a cold tingling feeling along his spine as Pete picked up two lengths of rope, each of them ending in a crude noose.

"When they find you both dangling from the rafters," Pete said. "And no way to tell how you got in here, or who did it, or how he got out. Believe me, this cottage will be a gold mine the rest of my life. I couldn't let you go. I just couldn't. Not when there's so much money at stake. Now we've talked long enough. I'll take you first."

He bent over Mr. Matthews, and Jeff closed his eyes, so he wouldn't have to look.

Consequently he missed seeing the teacher, who was lying on his back, bring his knees to his chest and then thrust his legs out in a terrific kick, which was not hampered at all by the fact his ankles were tied together.

His feet caught Pete Higgins in the stomach and the farmer was hurled away like a rock out of a catapult. Jeff heard his agonized gasp as the wind was driven out of him, and opened his eyes in time to see Pete crash against the far wall and slide to a sitting position on the floor.

Mr. Matthews sat erect and whipped his hands from behind him. In the time they had talked, he had managed to finish the job Jeff started. Now he grabbed a penknife from his pocket, slashed his feet free, and had Pete's hands and feet tied with the very nooses Pete had prepared for them.

A moment later Jeff was free, too, and standing up, a bit wobbly with relief.

"G-gosh," he said, when he could speak. "He was going to—to——"

"He certainly was," Mr. Matthews said, rubbing his wrists to get the circulation going. "And if his plan had succeeded, he'd probably have had wax dummies of us hanging from the rafters to give the sightseers goose flesh for years to come. Because I don't think anyone would have solved the mystery. His plan was so simple that it was actually fiendishly clever."

"Just to make this a real mystery cottage." Jeff swallowed with some difficulty. "Just so he could make some easy money."

"He's not normal on the subject of money. The idea of making so much so easily—let's just say it unbalanced him.

It's a good thing he came at me the way he did, or I couldn't have handled him. The strongest muscles in the body are in the legs and thighs, and he gave me a chance to use mine."

Pete Higgins was drawing long, shuddery breaths now, as he gradually regained the ability to breathe. Mr. Matthews watched him closely.

"Jeff, even though you haven't a license yet, I know you can drive a car. And this time it'll be all right for you to take mine and drive to town. Get your father to phone the State Police to come here. I'll stay to guard Pete. Your father can bring you back here and you two can rescue Harley Newcomb from the loft over the barn. He'll be mighty glad to see you."

"Yes, sir!" Jeff said and turned for the window. But even as he was crawling out, he had already come to a decision. He had decided not to try to write mystery stories. In the future he would just read them.

Sometimes a mystery writer's life could get awfully nerve-wracking!

_____

ALFRED HITCHCOCK SPEAKING: *Pete Higgins is now receiving free board and lodging and is very well satisfied. You see, someone told him how much income tax he would have had to pay if he had made a thousand dollars a week, and this helped him to realize the basic weakness in his whole scheme. As for Harley Newcomb, he has moved to England, where the roofs sit solidly on the ancient houses. He doesn't trust the American box-type house any more.*

Please observe that in this case we played fair with you. We told you how Pete loved money and we specified that he was Harley Newcomb's landlord. So you could easily have deduced that he was lying about the date he last saw the missing man. We mentioned the different sizes of shoes in Pete's possession, and we showed you the truck jack actually holding up a roof. If you de-duced that Pete was the man Harley Newcomb spoke to on the first day of the month, you may give yourself the rating of a ser-geant of detectives. If you deduced that he was responsible for the disappearance, you win the grade of lieutenant. If you also figured out the secret of the dwindling footsteps, promote yourself to captain. And if you penetrated the secret of the roof that could be lifted, you are entitled to be a full-fledged inspector. If, however, you missed all these points . . . Ahem. As you point out, the police missed them, too.

In closing The Mystery of the Man Who Evaporated, I have a suspicion that some of you are disappointed because it was not actually a case of black magic. I trust that in the future you will keep firmly in mind that there is no magic, and that tricks which seem magical will usually be found to be of the utmost simplicity when they are explained.

The Mystery of the Four Quarters

ALFRED HITCHCOCK SPEAKING: *I feel it is my solemn duty to warn you that there are a few long words in this story. I make this statement in the public interest, for the benefit of those who would rather go around the block than meet a long word face to face. For the others, there are also a small, plump spy, a large, ugly spy, a pair of twins who like riddles, a house where all the furniture is built half-size, and four pigeons —— But my sixty seconds are up. Without more ado, then, let us plunge into ——*

The Mystery of the Four Quarters

THE OLD HOUSE brooded among the trees at the crest of the hill like a witch thinking dark thoughts. It was a tall, thin house, crowned by a round room at the very top. This room had a round, peaked roof exactly like a witch's hat, and the two windows beneath it could have been her eyes.

Bettye Layton saw the resemblance as she and her twin brother, Nick, pushed their bicycles up the steep driveway. But when she mentioned it, Nick snorted.

"Girls!" he said. "To me it looks like a house, not a witch. I suppose you expect it to fly away on a broomstick."

Bettye would have been delighted if it had. But she sniffed even more scornfully than Nick.

"Boys! No imagination!"

"Girls!" Nick repeated, then added, "If you could ride a horse, we could have borrowed two from Uncle Jack and ridden here, instead of having to come on bikes. My legs are tired."

Bettye's legs were tired too. But she wouldn't admit it.

"Is it my fault I have an allergy to horses?" she asked. "And break out in great big hives when I get near one. Anyway, if you want to rest I'll wait for you."

Nick's answer was to race the rest of the way to the house. He leaned his bicycle against the steps, ran up to the front door, and whipped out a big brass key. Darting inside, he slammed the door in her face.

"That's not fair!" Outraged, Bettye pounded on the door. "I would have caught you but your legs are longer than mine."

Actually Nick was only an inch and a half taller. They looked very much alike, except that his light brown hair was cropped short and hers fell to her shoulders. Their blue eyes were very similar, shining with the same mixture of mischief, humor, and intelligence.

"What time is it if a clock strikes thirteen?" he called through the door. "If you can't answer you can't come in."

"It's time to have the clock repaired," Bettye called back, and Nick opened the door.

"I didn't think you knew that one," he said, grinning.

"It was easy," Bettye told him. "Actually I thought of two answers. The answer I like best is, 'It's midnight, Pacific Ghost Time.'"

"That's pretty good," Nick conceded. He closed the door. They looked around at the dimly lit interior—for all the shades were drawn—smelling the peculiar mixture of mustiness, dampness and dust which belongs exclusively to old, shut-up houses.

"I wonder how Peter Perkins knew about this house, way up here in Massachusetts," Nick said aloud. He took from his pocket a crumpled telegram and read it for the tenth time.

> *Nicholas Layton*
> *Bettye Layton*
> *c/o Mr. J. H. Joseph*
> *Forest Lake, Mass.*
>
> *Dear Young Friends:*
>
> *I have just learned that the old Blackwell mansion, in Gorset, near you, has a fine collection of old books of puzzles and riddles. Perhaps you can get to see them and make a list of them for me. I would like to buy them for my collection.*
>
> *Peter Perkins**

It had been sent from Atlantic Beach, where Peter Perkins was joke and puzzle editor of the Sunday paper. They had met Mr. Perkins two years earlier when spending the summer at Atlantic Beach, and found they shared a common fondness for puzzles and riddles. Nick and Bettye sent Peter any new ones they learned. They corresponded quite regularly. The thing that puzzled Nick was how Peter Perkins had ever heard of the curious old Blackwell mansion. Well, perhaps it was more famous than he realized, he decided, shoving the telegram back into his pocket.

---

*I'm sure you will recall that we met Peter Perkins in "The Mystery of the Seven Wrong Clocks." A. H.

Anyway, Luke Babbit, the real estate agent, had been glad to give them the key. Luke had muttered something about it being "purty peculiar" that two parties wanted to see the old mansion in the same month when years went by with nobody interested. But Nick hadn't paid any attention. If he had, he might have had some misgivings about their expedition.

"Look, Nick!" Bettye ran into the parlor and plopped herself down on a very small sofa, sending up a cloud of dust. "All the furniture is built about half size!"

"I know," Nick said, following her. He looked up at the ceiling, splotched with time and dampness. It was close enough to touch, and made him feel as if it were slowly going to settle down and crush him. "Mr. Amos Blackwell was a dwarf. But he was very rich, so a hundred years ago he had this house built with everything scaled to his size. Then he could walk around inside the house and feel as big as anybody."

"No wonder Mr. Babbit said no one will ever buy the house," Bettye remarked. She got up and dusted herself. "Goodness, it's dusty. We'd better go right up and look at the books. These low ceilings give me a funny feeling. As if I was Alice in Wonderland, when she started to grow big."

They started up the stairs. On the second floor were bedrooms with undersized beds and bureaus. They found the library in the round room on the third floor. This room had an extra-high ceiling, with bookshelves on all the wall space. There were dusty books scattered everywhere, though most were still on the shelves.

"Golly," Nick said. "Some of these books are in Greek and Latin."

"And French and German," Bettye added. "Mr. Blackwell must have been a terrific scholar. But here's an old book of riddles, puzzles and conundrums. Printed in

England, it says here in the front of the book."

"Let's look at it," Nick said. He preferred puzzles himself, because they required logical thinking. Bettye liked riddles best because a vivid imagination—which she certainly had—was a great help in solving riddles.

Bettye took the book from the shelf and blew the dust off it. Carrying it over to the window, through which the sunlight streamed, she opened it at random.

"Here's a riddle," she called. "Why is a room packed with married people like an empty room?"

Nick shook his head. "What's the answer?"

"Because there's not a single person in it."

They both dissolved in laughter. And at that precise moment they heard the strangely unexpected, and somehow frightening, sound of the front doorbell, downstairs.

They were instantly quiet. *Brrrring! Brrrring!* The bell clamored for attention. But who would be ringing the doorbell of a long-deserted old house in the woods, two miles from its nearest neighbor?

Of one accord they pressed close to the window. It gave them a fine view over the trees, across the valley and the river, as far as their aunt and uncle's summer hotel and farm, where they were spending the summer. But they couldn't see anyone down in the driveway below.

Again the doorbell rang, with a harsh sound that seemed to say, *Answer me!* It was an old-fashioned doorbell, not electric, with a handle outside the door. The unexpected caller was spinning this handle harder and harder, and the bell was ringing increasingly louder.

"I guess we'd better go see who it is," Bettye said, and Nick nodded. He led the way down the stairs. The bell was silent now, but to Nick the house seemed to be full of little echoes of it, coming from every corner. He shook himself impatiently. Now he was getting as imaginative as

Bettye!

He strode to the front door and jerked it open. A short, fat man stood there, beaming at them. He had a large mustache and very big spectacles, and he was wearing blue trousers and a blue coat with brass buttons. On his head sat a cap—much too small for him—which said *Western Union.*

"Telegram," the fat man said, holding out a yellow envelope to Nick. "For Mr. and Miss Layton, collec."

"Collect?" Nick asked puzzled.

"No, no." The man spoke English very well, but as if he were a foreigner who had studied it in England rather than in the United States. "Collec. That means collectively. For both of them together."

"He looks and talks like something out of *Alice in Wonderland,*" Bettye whispered. She and Nick had developed an ability to whisper to each other without moving their lips, and, in such a low voice they couldn't be heard from even a few feet away.

"How did he know we'd be here?" Nick whispered back.

"Curiouser and curiouser," Bettye whispered. "Open it and see what it says."

Nick opened the envelope and took out a sheet of yellow telegram paper. It said in a typed message:

> *Mr. Nicholas Layton*
> *Miss Bettye Layton*
> *The Old Blackwell Mansion*
> *Gorset, Mass.*
>
> *Dear Young Friends:*
>
> *Read me this riddle. I did not send you a telegram and yet I signed my name.*
> *Peter Perkins*

"Nick!" Bettye exclaimed. "This isn't a real telegram. It's just typed on a blank form someone got from a telegraph office!"

"That's right," Nick said. "And it says Peter Perkins didn't send us any telegram. That means——"

He looked at the small, fat man, who was still smiling. But now his smile had a curiously sinister quality and the ridiculous messenger cap perched on his head made him seem oddly menacing.

"This isn't a telegram," Nick said to him boldly. "And that other telegram, the one signed by Peter Perkins, wasn't from him at all, was it? And you aren't a telegraph messenger."

The fat man swept off his too-small cap and made a bow.

"Precisely," he said. "Exactly. Completely correct. On the nose. Please observe my command of the English language. I am happy to find you are both as alert and intelligent as I have heard. Accordingly you will realize that resistance is useless and might be dangerous."

"What is he talking about?" Bettye whispered. "He must be crazy."

"But he isn't," Nick whispered back. "He's looking at something in back of us. Turn around slowly, and don't scream or act scared."

"Do I ever?" In spite of the fact the words were whispered, Bettye's tone was icily indignant. Nick was tempted to remind her of the time she found a garter snake in her bed, but this wasn't the right moment.

They both turned around slowly to discover an ugly man with broad shoulders and long arms standing in the low-ceilinged hall. His head was bent because of his height, but he seemed about ten feet tall.

Actually he was only about six feet six, but he was big

enough to fill the passage completely.

Bettye gave a small gasp. Nick spoke quickly from the side of his mouth.

"When I count to three," he said, "start running—backwards! That will surprise them. We'll get past the fat man, grab our bikes and go down the hill as fast as we can. Now get ready. One—two—*three!*"

At the word *three* he ran backward with great force. Bettye ran too, but unfortunately she got confused and ran forward. She plunged against the big man, who simply grabbed her. Nick, running backward, hit the fat man's stomach alone. The short, stout stranger almost went over like a bowling pin. But he steadied himself and threw his arms around Nick. They were both caught as neatly as two butterflies pinned to a board.

"Goodness gracious!" The fat man puffed for breath. "They are quick! We mustn't give them another chance, Fritz."

"Twist their legs," the big man grunted, in some foreign accent Nick could not place. "Slow them down plenty."

"Now, Fritz, gentleness, kindness, that is our password. Or is it watchword? No matter. Let us take them to the truck."

He deftly shifted his grip so that he had Nick's wrist twisted behind Nick's back. It wasn't painful, but even a slight pressure could result in a broken wrist, and Nick knew it.

Bettye was staring at him, rigid in Fritz's grasp.

"Nick!" she said. "Do something!"

"There's nothing to do," Nick answered. "They're stronger than we are."

"A wise boy!" the fat man cried. "Bring the young lady, Fritz. But treat her as if you were escorting her to the opera."

He turned Nick around and directed him down the steps and along the driveway. Around the corner of the house was parked an old, enclosed truck on which was lettered, in new paint:

SAM WRIGHT
General Repair Work

Behind him, Nick heard Bettye shout.

"Help! Somebody, help! We——"

The words were cut off so abruptly Nick could visualize Fritz's large hand clamped over Bettye's mouth.

"Fritz!" Nick's captor said. "That is not nice. Take your hand away."

"She yell. She call help."

"Let her." The fat man turned Nick around so he could see Bettye's furious face. "Let them both yell. Come, shout for help. Both together. One—two—three——"

"Help!" Bettye yelled again. "Somebody, help!"

Seeing that Nick remained silent, she stopped.

"Why aren't you yelling?" she demanded.

"It isn't any use," Nick said. "Nobody can possibly hear us. They wouldn't let us yell if there was any chance of being heard."

"There you go," Bettye said bitterly, "being logical. Boys disgust me, always trying to be logical."

"A very interesting colloquy, meaning an informal conference or conversation," the small, fat man observed. "See, I know more English words than most Americans. I study it very hard. I know twelve languages, but English is the hardest. But get in. We have a large distance to go."

He took away Nick's wrist watch, his penknife with the compass set into the handle, his loose change, and the screwdriver he always carried because a screwdriver often comes in handy. The little man also took Bettye's small purse, but let her keep her silver bracelet with the lucky silver charm the size of a dime dangling from it. Then the two bundled Nick and Bettye into the closed truck, thrust their bicycles in after them, and locked the door at the back. Soon the truck drove away. There was a strong solid partition between them and the driver's seat, so they were very effectively imprisoned.

At first Nick tried to guess in what direction they were going, and for how long, by noting the turns they made and then counting his pulse to get the time they traveled before the next turn. But after a dozen turns he was completely confused and gave up.

"Where do you think they're taking us?" Bettye asked.

"We can't possibly guess," Nick said, in the logical tone that infuriated her. "Let's explore the truck and see if we can get out."

Together they examined every square inch of the truck's interior. All they discovered was a small crack near the bottom of the rear door. Nick, lying on his side and peering with one eye, could see a very narrow strip of the roadside. He watched, hoping to see some direction signs, but none were placed low enough.

Time passed and they got hungry, so they ate the lunches that were strapped into the baskets of their bicycles. Then, since they couldn't do anything else, they straightened out some burlap sacks on the floor of the truck and fell asleep.

How long they slept they had no idea, but they were awakened by a bump.

"Railroad tracks," Nick said, as they bumped again. He put his eye to the crack. He could just see the lower portions of many houses close together. "We're in some sort of large town or small city, I'd say," he reported. "Now we're

going over a bridge. There's a little river and I think I can see part of a brick factory building like they have in lots of old New England towns."

A moment later they turned into a narrow street, and then into a driveway. Nick's view was shut off as they entered a dark garage. The truck stopped, and Nick got to his knees.

"Keep calm," he told Bettye. "We have to find out what this is all about before we can make any plans."

It was the kind of advice Bettye considered entirely unnecessary, but which boys frequently gave to girls because they seemed to think girls were constantly in need of their superior wisdom. But she refrained from saying anything sarcastic. The truth was, in an emergency she usually preferred to depend on Nick's cool judgment rather than on her own sometimes sudden impulses.

A moment later the truck door opened. Fritz and the fat man stood there. Behind them the garage door was shut and locked.

"We have arrived," the fat man said brightly. "Welcome to my small domicile, meaning home or habitation. We will have some good talks and you will help me improve my English. I think I speak it too good, don't you? Not slangy enough, like real Americans."

As Bettye and Nick climbed out, he and Fritz took them by the arm and led them through a door. Beyond the door was a hall, then a flight of steps going down. They went down the stairs, then through another door. Fritz clicked a switch, and they found themselves in a basement room which, if not exactly luxurious, was tolerable enough.

It was a fairly large room, painted green, with a cement floor. Apparently it had been fitted up as a recreation room because two somewhat saggy studio couches were placed against opposite walls and in the middle of the floor was a ping-pong table with paddles and balls. A bookcase held a few old books. There was no window. Ventilation came from a small grilled opening high up in one wall.

"Make yourselves at home," the fat man said. "You shall have food and can play ping-pong and later we will converse, chat, talk, confer—what word would an American use?"

"Gab," Bettye suggested.

"Yak it up," Nick said at the same moment.

"Gab—yak it up." The man looked distressed. "Oh, American English is a very hard language. Well, come, Fritz, we have much to do."

They went out and the door was bolted on the outside.

"Now let's look the place over," Nick said.

That didn't take long. A tiny but adequate bath was attached to the recreation room, but there was nothing to be used for a tool and no apparent way to get out. They discovered that a standing, three-bulb lamp by the bookcase gave a more cheerful light than the overhead bulb, but aside from that, nothing at all suggested itself.

"I wish the switchbox we saw in the hall was in here," Nick muttered, but did not explain what he would have done with it if it had been. Bettye didn't ask because Nick didn't like to tell his ideas in advance. Some boys did, she had observed, but others liked to keep their ideas secret until the right moment came to use them. Nick was one of the latter.

"Now what do we do?" Bettye asked.

"Start crying," Nick told her.

"Crying?" She looked at him in amazement. "You know I only cry when I feel sad."

"Then feel sad," Nick ordered. "I hear someone coming down the steps, and by the sound it's Fritz."

Bettye was about to refuse, but Nick threw himself on a

couch and buried his face in his hands. Bettye flopped down on the other couch and thought of the time her pet kitten had wandered away and never come back. By the time the door opened and Fritz stamped in, bearing a tray of sandwiches and two glasses of milk, real tears were streaming down her cheeks.

Fritz put the tray on the ping-pong table.

"You two," he growled.

They sat up, Bettye weeping, Nick looking unhappy but not actually being able to cry. Somehow, Bettye realized, the sight of her tears made the big man feel better.

"Good," he said. "You act good. No smart tricks. Or——"

He gestured with his two hands as if wringing a neck, and made an ugly sound like bones breaking. Then he stalked out and bolted the door again. Instantly Bettye stopped crying.

"Well?" she asked her brother.

"Fritz doesn't trust us," Nick said, with a shade of satisfaction. "He's afraid we might be too clever for him. Seeing you cry reassured him. But the other one, the boss, is so proud of his own cleverness he's not worried about us."

"Well, if he isn't, I am," Bettye announced. "I want to get out of here."

"There are sheets on these couches, and I have an idea," Nick said. "But we have to wait until we find out what they are up to. Let's eat and see how much we can tell about them."

They helped themselves to sandwiches. By their appetites, they judged it must be late afternoon or early evening.

"They're foreigners," Bettye said. "I don't know what country, though. The fat one learned English well, but he studied a dictionary too much instead of living where English is spoken."

"And they went to a lot of trouble to catch us. The fact

they know Peter Perkins is our friend indicates they've either watched us a long time, or been reading our mail this summer."

"I'd say they've been reading our mail," Nick put in. "Uncle Jack and Aunt Ellen do run a summer hotel, and several of the guests seemed pretty foreign to me. One of them could easily have been spying on us and reading our mail."

"Which indicates a large organization," Bettye continued. "The way they found out we like puzzles, and then learned there were puzzle books in the old Blackwell house, and then had a false telegram sent to us from Atlantic Beach with Peter Perkins' name on it, all means that at least four or five people are working together. A foreign spy ring!" she finished, looking at Nick with large, round eyes.

"Catching us at the old Blackwell house, with no one else around, was very clever," Nick said. "They've gone to a lot of trouble. That means they want something big. But what? Dad isn't rich, and his chemical company certainly doesn't make anything awfully important, like rocket fuel or anything."

"Then what on earth can it be?" Bettye wrinkled her brows.

"We don't have to guess. They'll tell us pretty soon. The way the fat man acts, I don't think we have to worry about anything as long as they get what they want."

"Well, I'm pretty mad at them!" Bettye said. "I'd like to show them they can't go around playing tricks on us and get away with it!"

"So would I," Nick agreed. "We'll just have to wait and see what happens. Now how about some ping-pong?"

They played ping-pong for an hour with great verve. Nick was the steadier player but Bettye was more agile and could return shots that looked impossible. They were all even when the door opened and the little fat man came in. He had removed his false mustache and large glasses and funny clothes, and now looked like a businessman, or perhaps a teacher. No one who had seen him in his disguise would have an easy time recognizing him now, Nick thought.

"Oh, hello, Mr.—uh, is your name really Wright?" he asked.

"It's the name on my truck, but it isn't my real name," the man chuckled. "Wright is wrong. See? I can make jokes in English too. Call me Mr. Nemo. I have come to visit with you."

"Would you like to play ping-pong, Mr. Nemo?" Bettye asked politely.

"Oh, no thank you very muchly—I mean, very much." Mr. Nemo patted his plump stomach. "I only exercise my mind. Let us try something else. Tell me a riddle. Let me test my large knowledge of your language."

"Here's an easy one," Bettye told him. "Why does everybody put on the right shoe first?"

"The right shoe first?" Mr. Nemo looked down at his feet. "Yes, indeed so, I do put on the right shoe first. But I don't know why. What is the answer?"

"Because it would be silly to put on the wrong shoe first," Bettye told him.

"You should have guessed that one because we were just talking about right and wrong," Nick said.

"Oh, indeed I should," Mr. Nemo agreed. "One more, please."

"Here's one I made up," Nick said. "Why is a foolish man like a bunch of artificial flowers and a counterfeit dollar?"

Mr. Nemo looked very blank. Even Bettye scowled as she pondered.

"I know!" she cried at last. Mr. Nemo shook his head. "But I do not. You will have to tell me."

"Because none of them have any sense," Bettye told him. Still he looked bewildered.

"Please?"

"A foolish man doesn't have any s-e-n-s-e." Nick spelled it out. "Artificial flowers don't have any s-c-e-n-t-s. And a counterfeit dollar is worthless so it doesn't have any c-e-n-t-s."

"Sense—scents—cents," Mr. Nemo murmured. "Dear me, English is very difficult. I think I know enough already, so let us get down to business. It is really most simple. Your father has something I want. I tried to steal it from him. I failed. Now I will make him a trade for it. I will trade him you."

He beamed at them as if he had just done them a great favor. Nick and Bettye exchanged an I-told-you-so glance.

"I'm sure there will be no trouble," Mr. Nemo said. "I have planned so very well. Please read this letter."

He took a folded sheet of paper from his pocket and gave it to Nick. Bettye crowded close to read it too. It was addressed to their father.

> *Dear Mr. Layton:*
>
> *Recently you have invented a new and very effective rust remover and preventer. I would much like to have the formula. I am desirous of bringing the benefits of your wonderful invention to my own country.*
>
> *You will write out the formula and photograph it very small on microfilm. I will send you four messengers and you will give one copy to each. Within twenty-four hours after they return, Nicholas and*

Bettye will be telling you all about their adventure. But only if you follow exactly the instructions that will accompany messengers and do not call the authorities in any way. I am a kind man but I am firm. Your children's fingerprints you will find below as evidence they are with me and in good health.

Yours truly and sincerely,

Mr. Nemo

Nick looked at Mr. Nemo, his expression puzzled.

"I don't understand," he said. "Rust remover? I mean if dad had invented a new rocket fuel or something like that——"

"Rocket fuels!" Mr. Nemo said, waggling his head. "I am not interested in rocket fuels, my boy. I am a businessman. Stop to think! How many millions of pounds of iron and steel rust every year! How many men spend all their time painting great bridges and oiling machines so they won't rust! How many millions of machines of all kinds get rusty and are worthless each year!"

Nick looked impressed. "That's right," he said to Bettye. "Remember when the garage leaked one winter, and our power mower got rusty and had to be thrown away? That's when dad started working on his rust preventative. And do you realize our bikes haven't shown a speck of rust since we rubbed on that stuff he gave us last fall?"

"The war against rust costs millions of dollars!" Mr. Nemo said. "In my country we have many expensive machines that get rusty because the farmers leave them out in the fields. Soon they are worthless. Your father's new rust preventer will save them for us."

"Then why don't you just buy it from him, instead of stealing the formula?" Nick asked.

"Wouldn't that be a lot simpler?" Bettye inquired.

"Yes," Mr. Nemo agreed. "But much more expensive. We will probably use at least a million dollars' worth of the formula in just one year."

"Golly!" Nick exclaimed to Bettye. "A million dollars' worth! No wonder they have gone to so much trouble. You're a spy, aren't you?" he asked Mr. Nemo.

"Now please." Mr. Nemo took an ink pad from his pocket. "Touch this and put your fingerprints on the letter. I am not spy—at least not official spy. Most unofficial. That is better way."

Nick put his hands in his pockets. Bettye put hers behind her back.

"You don't think that would convince dad, do you?" asked Nick.

"Dad is a scientist. He needs proof of everything," Bettye added.

"And two fingerprints won't prove that we are really all right," Nick said darkly.

"Please!" Mr. Nemo looked distressed. "My plan is so perfect, and you are in no danger. No one can possibly trace us here. And later, even though you describe us, we will be ten thousand miles away and it will not matter."

"They might follow your messengers," Nick said. "That's the weak point in every scheme like this."

"Sit down," said Mr. Nemo. He turned and opened the door. "Fritz! Bring me Dancer, Prancer, Donder and Blitzen!"

Nick and Bettye sat on a couch. In a moment Fritz appeared, carrying a wicker basket. Mr. Nemo took it and dismissed him. Then from the basket he drew out a sleek gray pigeon, which he cradled carefully in his hands.

"This is Dancer," he said. "Is he not handsome? Prancer, Donder and Blitzen are his brothers."

"A homing pigeon!" Nick exclaimed, his face lighting up with interest. "You're going to have four homing pigeons bring you the copies of the formula on microfilm! That's pretty clever."

"I think so," Mr. Nemo said. "They have been carefully trained. They will be delivered by express, and your father will be instructed to release them exactly an hour and a half before sunset tomorrow. They will then bring me lovely present. That is why I gave them name of your Santa Claus' reindeers.

"You are thinking your father might try to follow them, but that is impossible. They will fly at a speed close to sixty miles an hour, and at that time of day great flocks of birds, pigeons and starlings, are in the sky, returning to the cities from the country where they have been feeding. My four pretty pigeons will be quickly lost among them all. The only danger is from a hawk, perhaps. But all four can not be lost."

He smoothed the bird's feathers.

"You see? Even if one or two of my birds are lost, the rest will return. No one will pay attention. Many men in this town raise and train pigeons for a hobby, and we have been here for months, so everyone is used to us. There is nothing to attract attention, nothing. Dancer and Prancer, and perhaps Donder and Blitzen, will return with the formula. Fritz and Mr. Nemo leave in the old truck, transfer to a car, go to an airport, and fly away like birds themselves.

"Soon after, you and your father are reunited. A friendly business transaction has been completed with a minimum of fuss and bother. And I am not really taking anything away from him. He still has his formula for his business. I am simply sharing it with him."

"It looks like he's thought of everything," Nick said,

grudgingly, to Bettye. "I guess we'll have to coöperate."

"I guess so. But Mr. Nemo, you'd better let us write something to daddy in our own handwriting. Then he'll know we're fine and won't hesitate about sending the formula."

"Very good," Mr. Nemo said. "But you must write fast and not try any foolish tricks. Mr. Nemo is not a man to be truffled with."

"Trifled with," Bettye corrected him. "Certainly not."

Mr. Nemo put the letter on the ping-pong table and handed Bettye a pen.

"Write fast," he warned. "If you stop I will think you are trying a trick. I know you are clever. Do not be too clever."

"My goodness, how clever can we be?" Bettye grumbled. "If we were really clever we wouldn't be here at all."

And she wrote swiftly at the bottom of the letter:

Dear Daddy:

Please do exactly what Mr. Nemo says and I know we'll be All Right! He's a nice man and has treated us fine. If you get time, telephone Mabel Jones and ask her about Lovey-Dove, the pony she promised to sell me. She telephoned two nights ago and said it was lame and seemed to have strained a muscle in her forequarters. Maybe you could get a doctor to observe Lovey-Dove's forequarters and make sure she is All Right.

Also be sure my tropical fish have their water changed, and go to the kennels and tell Rex I miss him. May I have a budgie? Auntie has a budgie and they are awfully cute. We miss you.

Your loving daughter,
Bettye

Mr. Nemo read the letter slowly, out loud. Then he nodded.

"Very good," he said. "I am glad you did not try any clever tricks. Now my boy, it is your turn."

"All right," Nick said. He wrote as fast as he could move the pen.

> *Dear Dad,*
>
> *Girls are certainly silly! Imagine worrying about animals at a time like this! And who ever heard of naming a pony Lovey-Dove? Even for a girl that's pretty icky. Tell her she has to let the name stay Peggy. Peggy's as good a name for a girl pony as any. Anyway, though, she's right when she says we are all right. Mr. Nemo's a right guy, and if you follow the directions I know you will find us waiting for you.*
>
> *Love,*
>
> *Nick*

Mr. Nemo now read his letter out loud, and at a certain phrase he turned to scowl at Nick.

"This 'right guy,'" he said. "I don't like the sound of it."

"It means you're an okay Joe," Bettye told him.

"A jolly good fellow," Nick put in, selecting a very old-fashioned term Mr. Nemo might have heard of.

"Oh, a jolly good fellow!" Mr. Nemo's face brightened. "I understand. But 'right guy,' and 'okay Joe.'" He shook his head. "I do not think English is a sensible language. Well, never mind. Your father will have this in the morning. And I do hope he follows directions exactly. Then we will all be well and happy."

With a big smile he went out, bolting the door. As soon

as he was gone Bettye plumped herself down beside Nick.

"Your message to daddy was very good," she whispered. "Of course I was counting on you to help make mine clearer. I could only say so much. Still, mine was rather good too, don't you think?"

"It was all right," Nick said, without enthusiasm.

"What do you mean, all right?" Bettye demanded. "It was very good! Don't you think daddy will catch it?"

"I expect he will," Nick agreed. "Only I'm not sure it was a good idea to begin with. If you hadn't put a secret message in your letter, I wasn't going to. But you did so I had to help make it clearer. But I had other ideas."

"What other ideas?" Bettye asked, curiously.

But Nick wouldn't tell her. All he would say was, "Tonight we'd better go to bed early. We have a lot to do tomorrow."

Good evening. Perhaps you thought I had business elsewhere this time. But I assure you I have been following events with great interest. It seems obvious that the apparently innocent messages Nick and Bettye wrote say a great deal more than they seem to. I don't blame Mr. Nemo for not catching on. After all, there are one or two things he doesn't know. For instance, go back and read paragraph eight at the very beginning of our story. This should remind you of something which will aid you in unraveling Bettye's message. For another clue—what else has four quarters? (Never mind how it is spelled.) A dollar, yes. But what else? The four quarters of the globe, of course. And the four quarters of a——?

As for Nick's hidden message, read aloud quickly the words, "Peggy's as good a name as any." What word do you get from the combination of the first two words there, and what does it suggest to you? Particularly when he adds, "follow the directions." But if I say any more, I'll be spilling the works, to use the quaint argot of the underworld. So on with the story!

After that the time went quickly. Fritz brought them supper, on plastic plates with plastic cutlery. After supper Bettye teased Nick to tell her about his idea, but Nick was stubbornly silent. They played ping-pong until Nick abruptly decided it was time for bed.

They washed in cold water in the tiny bath and tumbled into bed with most of their clothes on. The two studio couches were made up with clean sheets under the green couch covers. Both fell asleep swiftly.

Because it was dark in the basement room, with no window, they slept late. They woke when Fritz unlocked the door to bring in breakfast. Nick switched on the three-bulb standing lamp and they sat up yawning. Mr. Nemo came in as Fritz put down the tray of bacon and eggs and milk.

"Dancer and Prancer and Donder and Blitzen have been delivered," Mr. Nemo announced, rubbing his smooth, soft hands together. "I hope, I do hope your father follows directions and releases my four messengers from his factory roof all together just an hour and a half before sunset today."

Nick and Bettye gave each other a look of dismay. They hadn't known the pigeons were supposed to be released all together, at the same spot. In fact, their messages to their father had definitely suggested he release the pigeons from four different spots far apart!

"I have a colleague—English word meaning associate or ally—in your father's factory watching to see if any monkey tricks are tried," he informed them. "Oh, I do hope not so."

"The word is monkeyshines," Bettye told him. "And I'm sure daddy will do exactly as you said."

"We will see," Mr. Nemo said. As soon as he and Fritz went out, the twins held a whispered conference.

"Golly, suppose someone telephones Mr. Nemo and tells

him that daddy isn't following the directions?" Bettye asked.

"We can count on dad. But just the same we're going to try my plan too."

"Well, what is it?"

"You'll see. As soon as we've eaten and Fritz has taken these plastic plates away."

Nick would say no more, most irritatingly, but as soon as Fritz had removed the breakfast things he sprang into action. In the small bath was a tiny mirror. He broke it with the heel of his shoe and carefully picked out a large, sharp sliver of glass. Next he took the sheets off both couches and had Bettye smooth back the covers so they looked made.

Now began a long, difficult job of using the sharp glass to cut the sheets into strips of cotton cloth several inches wide. When he had all the strips he could get, he told Bettye. "Now we're going to weave ropes. You do it better so it's your job. I'll play ping-pong. They'll hear the ball and won't suspect anything."

After a first protest, Bettye settled down to weaving four ropes, six feet long, from the torn strips. Nick batted the ping-pong ball from the table to the cement wall, where it bounced back again, giving quite a convincing imitation of two players.

When they heard Fritz bringing lunch, they hid the strips of cloth and partly woven ropes under a couch, pretending to be tired from a morning of exercise. Fritz only looked at them and grunted, apparently unsuspicious.

As soon as Fritz had cleared away the lunch dishes, they started again.

"You're going too slowly," Nick criticized. "I'll have to help."

"It was your idea," Bettye reminded him.

Between them, they managed to weave four fairly tight

ropes, six feet long. Then Nick put a running noose in the end of each one. Bettye thought they looked fine, but Nick scowled with dissatisfaction.

"It's no good," he said. "It won't work."

"What won't work?" Bettye asked. Nick had still not explained his plan.

"We aren't strong enough to overcome two grown men with these," Nick said. "Anyway, they're too short."

"Well, what can we do?" Bettye found she had been counting heavily on Nick's idea, whatever it might be.

Nick scowled harder. Then he grinned.

"I have it!" he exclaimed. "I've just invented a brand-new weapon. The first important new way to use a rope since the lariat was invented."

Bettye thought this was a rather big boast, but she didn't say so. Nick took two of the ropes and tied the free ends together. Then he tied the other two together. Now he had two ropes, each about six feet long, and each with two nooses—one at either end.

"The double-noosed lariat!" he said. "Golly, I wish I could patent it!"

"If we're not strong enough to handle Fritz and Mr. Nemo with four ropes," Bettye said, "I don't see how we can do it with two."

"You will," Nick promised. "Oh, oh, here comes Mr. Nemo. Quick, hide the ropes."

They got the ropes under the couch just in time. Mr. Nemo came in looking severe.

"I have had a phone call from my friend in your father's factory," he told them. Nick and Bettye waited, their hearts beating fast.

"He tells me"—Mr. Nemo paused—"that your father has just released Dancer and Prancer and Donder and Blitzen from the roof of his factory, and they are on the way. They should be here in less than an hour."

"I told you daddy would coöperate," Bettye said.

"Supper will be delayed. I will be very busy. As soon as my messengers arrive, we must leave."

"Leave?" Nick asked. "Where?"

"To another place where I have a little laboratory. Naturally I must test the formula. Oh, I do hope it is the right one." And clucking his tongue, Mr. Nemo went out.

"Daddy will send the right formula, won't he?" Bettye asked. Nick nodded.

"Of course. But just the same, we must be ready. Now, to get us to the truck will take both of them, and when they come in the room this is what we have to do——"

He whispered his plan, and Bettye's eyes grew wider and wider. Part of it involved sacrificing the silver lucky charm on her bracelet, but she let him pull it loose without a protest.

Nick unscrewed one bulb in the three-bulb standing lamp and carefully put the silver charm down inside the socket. Then he screwed the bulb back in, but only part way.

Next he got out the two double-noosed ropes and straightened them out, then slid them under the couch at their feet, so he and Bettye could pull them out fast. After that they waited, with growing restlessness, until they heard a tiny bell ring somewhere above them. A moment later it rang again.

"That's a signal," Nick whispered. "Two pigeons have entered the pigeon cote that must be up on the roof. Any minute now Fritz and Mr. Nemo will be coming."

In less than five minutes, the door opened and the two men stepped in.

"Come along, children," Mr. Nemo said. "Dancer and Blitzen are back. We have two microfilm copies of your father's wonderful formula. Now we are leaving."

"We aren't going," Nick said.

"We'd rather stay here," Bettye added in a small voice.

"See?" Fritz grunted. "I tell you they make trouble. But I handle them."

"Gently, Fritz," Mr. Nemo said, as the two men strode toward the couch where Nick and Bettye sat. "Take the boy. I'll get the girl to the truck."

"Come, boy!" Fritz stood in front of Nick and reached out long arms. But Nick wasn't there. He ducked down and grabbed an end of one rope from beneath the couch. Jumping up close to the surprised man, he threw the ready noose over Fritz's head, then pulled it tight.

"Quick, Bettye!" he called, diving for the second rope.

Bettye was coöperating as smoothly as if they had had hours of practice. She had the other end of the same, double-noosed rope in her hand. As Mr. Nemo looked in amazement at Nick and Fritz, she jumped up and slipped her noose over Mr. Nemo's head, then pulled it tight.

Now—though the two men did not yet realize it—they were tied together by a rope with two nooses that would tighten harder the more they struggled to pull apart.

Fritz was not bothered at first. He yelled with anger and tried again to grab Nick. But Nick was down on his knee, holding the second rope. As Fritz lifted a big foot, Nick slid the noose over it and pulled it tight around the ankle. Fritz, grunting savagely, turned around. As he did so he naturally pulled on the rope which bound him and Mr. Nemo together, neck to neck.

Mr. Nemo, squealing like a frightened piglet, fell down at the sudden jerk on his neck. Bettye got the other noose over one of his legs. And while Fritz pulled at the rope around his throat, jerking Mr. Nemo with every pull and making the little fat man screech louder than ever, Nick jumped up.

He ran to the lamp and screwed the loose light bulb tightly down on top of the silver charm which was in the socket.

There was a hiss, and suddenly all the light in the basement and first floor of the house turned to darkness as the short circuit in the lamp blew out the fuse in the main switchbox. The basement room was now pitch dark.

"Bettye—the door!" Nick shouted.

They had both memorized where the door was, and they headed for it blindly. There was a great crash as Fritz, threshing around wildly in the darkness, fell over Mr. Nemo. Nick fell over them both, but evaded grasping hands and crawled the rest of the way to the door, where he bumped into Bettye's legs.

He stood up. Behind them the two men were rolling and struggling to get loose from the ropes, not realizing, in the darkness, that each was anchored to the other, so that every move one made hindered the other's efforts to get loose.

Nick and Bettye groped their way out the door, then closed and bolted it. Outside they listened for a moment to the thuds and bumps and cries from the two men tied together inside.

"Nick, it's a wonderful invention!" Bettye whispered. "It's positively stupendous."

"We couldn't handle them," Nick answered. "But by making them fight each other, we didn't have to. Now let's find the stairs."

In the darkness they felt their way to the stairs and up. On the first floor there was still enough daylight coming in the windows to enable them to see where they were going. They dashed toward the front door, and an instant later were standing on the street, looking around at rows of small brick houses and the unfamiliar skyline of a strange city.

As they stood there, a crowded sedan came speeding up the street and stopped. Uncertain whether it might be friend or foe, Nick and Bettye were all set to run when a tall, familiar form leaped out.

"Nick!" he called. "Bettye!"

"Dad! . . . Daddy!" They raced joyfully to him.

As soon as they had gotten over their astonishment and relief, the twins told their father about Fritz and Mr. Nemo in the basement. Immediately the other men in the car took their flashlights and went down to capture the two.

"And be careful," Bettye said. "I'm afraid Fritz is rather cross by now."

"I just hope," Nick said in a thoughtful tone, "that he hasn't broken Mr. Nemo's neck, trying to get loose."

The story is so nearly finished that it seems quite unnecessary to interrupt and ask you how Mr. Layton happened to arrive so opportunely at exactly the right spot. Surely by now you have managed to decipher the true meaning of those odd-sounding messages. If not, it's a good thing you weren't responsible for Nick and Bettye's rescue. In any event, for those—like Mr. Nemo—who insist on having everything spelled out, kindly turn to page 202, where the mystery is explained simply enough for even an adult to understand.

CONCLUSION

"But I do not understand." Mr. Nemo's large brown eyes were sorrowful and puzzled. Stick-on bandages adorned his forehead and chin, and there was a bandage around his throat, which he touched tenderly from time to time. He sat stiffly on a chair in the hotel room Mr. Layton had engaged, facing Nick and Bettye and their father. A large, neatly dressed man stood guard at the door.

"My plan was so clever," Mr. Nemo said. "Everything went just right. You released my pigeons from your factory just as I directed. Yet you were outside my door almost as soon as the pigeons arrived back."

He looked at Nick and Bettye.

"I understand how you tied Fritz and me together," he said. "It was clever . . . but it was unkind. Truly I was not going to hurt you."

"Oh, we trusted you, Mr. Nemo," Nick said. "But we didn't trust Fritz. And anyway, we couldn't let you steal dad's formula, could we? So we told dad how to get your pigeons to lead him and the F.B.I. men right to you."

"But that can not be," Mr. Nemo protested. "Four pigeons—no one could keep them in sight for fifty miles, among thousands of other birds, even from an airplane."

"We didn't try to," Mr. Layton told him. "When your lookout, for I'm sure you had one, phoned to tell you he had seen me release four pigeons from the roof of my factory, he didn't realize he had really seen someone else made up to look like me. The pigeons were different, too. You see, as soon as the pigeons and your instructions arrived, together with the messages from my children, the authorities and I got very active.

"We found someone who looked like me, and smuggled him into the factory with a basket of pigeons to release at the right time. When that was taken care of, we made other plans for the real pigeons.

"We got the F.B.I. on the job, and arranged to have each of the four pigeons released separately from places many miles apart. As soon as they were released, they circled around, got their direction, and headed straight for home.

"When they did that, men with telescopes and compasses marked the exact direction of their flight. They all flew northwest, but at different angles because they were starting from different spots. Their flight paths were phoned to me and the F.B.I. agents at the Boston airport. We plotted the four directions in pencil on a large map. Now naturally, since all four pigeons were heading for this city, the four lines came together here."

"Yes, I understand that," Mr. Nemo said. "Elementary matter of direction finding. But I do not know how you thought of it, or how in this entire city you came straight to my house."

Mr. Layton chuckled.

"As soon as we had the destination spotted," he said, "the F.B.I. men and I took off in a plane for here. Another F.B.I. man got the local chief of police on the phone and asked him to find out anything he could about a man, probably a foreigner and probably using the name of Wright, who might have moved to this city recently and who engaged in training pigeons for a hobby. By the time we got here, the police had your name and address for us. Sam Wright, General Repairs."

"That was I," Mr. Nemo said. "Or should I say, that

was me? English still confuses me."

"It was you, either way," Mr. Layton told him. "We drove straight to your house just in time to see Nick and Bettye coming out."

"And just in time to save me from being strangled by Fritz," Mr. Nemo said. "But I still can not understand how your children sent you any information. I read their letters myself. They were quite simple, childish letters."

"You should read them again," Mr. Layton said. "I have rather smart children, I'm happy to say." He winked at Nick and Bettye. "Anyway, you'll have quite a number of years to figure out the messages, so I'll see you get copies of their letters when you are finally settled in your new residence. I'll give you one clue—my daughter is allergic to horses, so when she started talking about buying a horse, I naturally understood she meant me to disregard what she seemed to be saying and to look for some other information she was trying to give me."

Mr. Nemo stood up.

"Thank you," he said. "Anyway, I will have chance to study American English better."

"I have a new riddle for you before you go, Mr. Nemo," Bettye said. "What has two heads and four eyes and four legs and can't see or walk?"

Mr. Nemo looked at her sadly.

"I can guess answer," he said. "Fritz and me tied together in a dark cellar by clever twins."

He heaved a deep sigh and walked out the door the F.B.I. man held open for him.

"Poor fellow," Mr. Layton said. "I'm afraid you made him feel pretty riddle-iculous, the way you turned his pigeons into stool pigeons."

Nick and Bettye groaned loudly. But there was nothing they could do about it. Nick liked puzzles and Bettye liked riddles. But their father's hobby was puns.

ALFRED HITCHCOCK SPEAKING: *It looks very much as if Nick and Bettye and their father have left me the task of explaining the messages the twins slipped into their letters. Of course most of you have already deciphered them and can skip this part, but I shall not shirk my duty. For the benefit of those who came in late, I will explain all. First, however, go back and read again the letters Nick and Bettye wrote, to refresh your memory. While you are doing that, I will take the opportunity to note that in due time the other members of Mr. Nemo's little organization were caught and properly dealt with.*

Now as to the messages. As Mr. Layton pointed out, Bettye is allergic to horses. So when she speaks of buying a horse named Lovey-Dove, and asks her father to have its forequarters carefully observed, it is plain enough she is talking about something else. Lovey-Dove sounds, at first, merely like a sentimental name. But when there are pigeons in the case, as there are here, anyone who thinks for a moment will realize that a pigeon is a form of dove and Bettye must be talking about the pigeons.

Pigeons, though, do not have forequarters, and it is the pigeons we are interested in. What does Bettye really mean? The word forequarters suggests to almost anyone except a foreigner, like Mr. Nemo, who has learned his English from books, the words four quarters. What has four quarters? A dollar—but that doesn't fit. The globe has four quarters. And a compass has four quarters. Mr. Layton sees that Bettye wants him to connect the pigeons somehow with the four quarters of the compass. A little thought gives him her idea—release the pigeons each from a different quarter of the compass, or at least a good distance from each other, and observe the direction in which they fly to get back home. Which is what he did.

Bettye also twice used the words All Right, capitalized. This seemed to have some meaning. When in Nick's letter Mr. Layton came across the phrase "Mr. Nemo's a right guy," he knew it was no accident. He deduced the twins were telling him their captor used the name of Wright. And as Mr. Nemo's letter was obviously written by a foreigner, Mr. Layton, as soon as he knew what city the pigeons were heading for, could have someone phone ahead to ask the police for information about a foreigner using the name of Wright, and training pigeons.

Just to be more helpful, Nick also drew his father's attention to the words "Peggy's as good a name as any." But the first two words in that sentence, spoken swiftly, sound like "Pegasus." And Pegasus of course was the flying horse of mythology. Today's flying horse, I think you will agree, is the airplane. When Nick added, "if you follow the directions I know you will find us waiting for you," it was rather clear that he was suggesting his father use a plane to follow the direction given him by the homing pigeons and rescue them. Of course, Mr. Layton could undoubtedly have figured out the best way to reach them for himself, but Nick didn't believe in taking any chances.

I am sure the foregoing explanation will make everything clear to you. If you have any questions, please reread the story and I am certain all will be crystal clear. It wouldn't be any use in asking Nick or Bettye. Nick is experimenting with a three-noosed lariat, and Bettye is making up a book of original riddles. I don't believe it will catch on, however—some of them have triple meanings.

But now that we have concluded "The Mystery of the Four Quarters," I must say good night. I hope you have enjoyed our little excursion into suspense and detection as much as I have. And I sincerely trust you will guard with tightly locked lips the answers to the mysteries we have recounted. As I suggested in our Introduction, let your friends find out the answers the hard way—make them read the book!

ALFRED HITCHCOCK